COASTAL CULPRIT

COASTAL ADVENTURE SERIES 7

DON RICH

Library of Congress PCN Data

Rich, Don

Coastal Culprit/Don Rich

Florida Refugee Press LLC

Cover by: Cover2Book.com

Published by FLORIDA REFUGEE PRESS, LLC, 2021

Crozet, VA

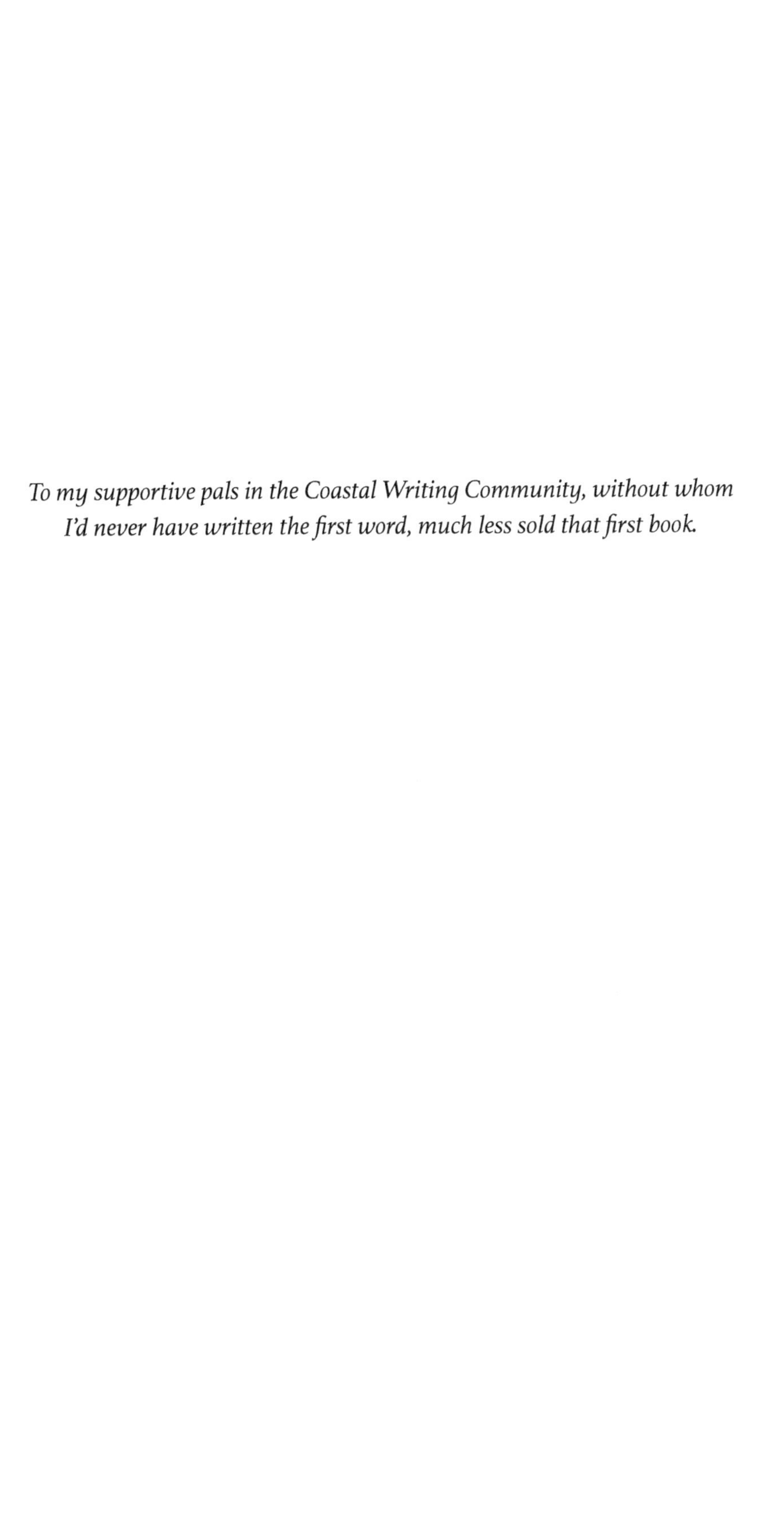

To my supportive pals in the Coastal Writing Community, without whom I'd never have written the first word, much less sold that first book.

PROLOGUE

Two months ago...

Martin "The Mole" Stoneman was sitting in the passenger seat closest to the door of Shaw Air's Cessna Citation CJ3 jet. He was on the return leg of a charter from Virginia Beach to Pennsylvania and back. The Mole earned his nickname because of his continual squinting and blinking under the harsh glare of television studio lights. Nobody dared call him that to his face, but within his industry, this was what he was more commonly known as, albeit behind his back.

This had been a quick trip to tour a factory that produces sample-sized plastic pouches of liquids. They packaged everything from shampoo to food condiments; the latter was even certified kosher. Not that this mattered to the Mole; what he was up to was not kosher or even authentic. The truth was he didn't even plan to deal with the company that owned that plant much longer, even though they were the country's top producer of these types of products. The Mole had only been dealing with them so that he could steal information to start his small production line. Unbeknownst to the factory owners, he was installing similar but smaller packaging equipment in a building on the southern part of the Eastern Shore of Virginia, an area more commonly known as ESVA. But instead of relish, mayonnaise, or shampoo, the Mole packaged false hope, and it had already started making him a fortune. Or rather, *another* fortune.

He glanced to his right, seeing his son, Martin "Marty" Junior, in the seat across the narrow aisle from his. The young man was preoccupied with his thoughts. How the Mole wished that his son had more of an aptitude for the family business. He knew though he'd have no choice but to continue bringing him along as his heir apparent, at least for the short run. Marty would be seen as the next face of this "business" that was so dependent on looks, and even more on presence. Even though things in their occupation had begun to slowly change, for thousands of years it had been men that had been the leaders, with very few exceptions. And so, the plan had been that the mantle would first fall to Marty. But he and Marty had been clashing more and more frequently, mostly about the direction of their business; they had some very large fundamental differences that were starting to become insurmountable.

His daughter Sandra, riding in the seat immediately behind his, was so much better suited to the business side of what they did. How he wished that Marty could be more like his sister. It was she who had recognized this as the perfect time to pivot, that the time had been ripe to sell their cable TV show and move into other areas before the value started to decline. Not only that, but she had identified and dealt with the group that was purchasing it, and she had also found her father's replacement host to add to the package. She created the training schedule they had followed last year, while they groomed the talented and charismatic young man named Peter. He had a rapidly rising television rating, and she liked the irony of his name. The show's ranking had been on the rise at that time as well, bolstering their asking price and the eventual terms. But she knew what the market didn't, that there was some new and hefty competition on the horizon that would bring some big changes to that marketplace.

And along the way her father had gotten burned out with the

time demands that a five-day-per-week live show had put on his life. Maybe it wouldn't have been as bad if he still fully believed in the "product" they pushed on the show, but she couldn't remember back to the time when he did. It had been before her mother died, and prior to him considering television, well before the money had gotten so big and his ego had grown to match it. Before his true faith had faded, leaving him now rich but hollow.

He had developed this new "product concept" about the time that his daughter convinced him to sell the show. The stars had seemed to align for them, and the Mole saw that she was right; it was time to cash out of a show that was probably close to the top of its market value. In addition to the money, the show had given him widespread fame, and like so many other older famous people, he was now leveraging that fame as he decided to push other products. Only instead of bathtubs with doors, reverse mortgages or precious metals, he sold the most desirable of all products: hope for the human condition. He sold it to those who had little or none. They were the ones who wanted and needed it so desperately and would do almost anything to obtain it. They would pay whatever they could afford and even what they couldn't. Because of his celebrity, they were willing to believe whatever he said, which is what he counted on. His faith having long ago been replaced by indifference and greed, he now had little, if any, conscience left.

They landed and taxied to the tarmac in front of the private terminal, their car pulled up next to the airstair door as they stopped. One of the workers from the private terminal greeted him as he exited the airplane, undoubtedly recognizing him from television.

"Have a good flight, reverend?"

He squinted as he smiled and replied in his practiced televangelist voice with its trademark cadence and false enthusiasm, "It's always a good flight when you're doing God's work, son."

1

SALTWATER GOSPEL

P *resent day...*

I MADE my way down the docks from the *Mallard Cove Yacht Brokerage* office past the *Cove Restaurant* and charter boat row. I was headed to the *Cove Beach Bar and Grill* to grab a bite of lunch. Despite it being early fall, the warmer than usual weather was keeping this and *Mallard Cove's* other beach bar, *The Catamaran*, almost as busy as a mid-summer Saturday, and open tables are hard to come by. I spotted my new friend, Reverend Eddie Jones, at the far corner table. Eddie, more commonly known around ESVA as "Rev", had seen me looking around and waved me over, pointing to an empty seat across the table. I weaved through the crowd with a large young white Labrador retriever behind me on a leash. Our open-air facility is dog-friendly.

"I'd say you're doing pretty well here when the owner can't even get a table," Rev remarked as I sat down.

My fiancée, Lindsay Davis, and I are the majority owners of the *Mallard Cove Marina* complex. Along with a handful of partners, in a little under three years, we've created the hottest spot on the

I

southern tip of ESVA, with four restaurants/bars, a hotel, a modern marina, in-and-out boat storage, and our latest addition, a yacht brokerage. It was there I'd been spending a lot of time lately.

"Can't complain, Rev. How about you? How's your 'flock' these days?" Rev is the minister at the Waterman's Church of ESVA.

"We can always make room in a pew for you, Murph."

"Uh, well, Sundays are kind of busy around here, Rev. and my 'church' has always been out on the water. You know that song by the Eli Young Band, 'Saltwater Gospel?' It could've been written about me. But I'll still be sure to make it to your service this Easter."

Rev laughed. He knew that I wasn't a real candidate for his weekly services, but he wanted me to know I'm always welcome. He's well aware that attending is a choice no one could make for anyone else who had already reached their teen years or beyond.

"I'll make sure we save you a spot here on your beach for that sunrise service. It was great of you to volunteer to let us use it."

"Uh, yeah. It's a nice coincidence that we have a clear view of the sunrise out between the islands on Easter every year, Rev. And I'll be here for that one."

"Murph, it's been my experience that there are no *co*-incidences, but there are a lot of *God*-incidences."

Rev had a great way of putting you at ease, whether or not you were a believer. With anyone else, it might have been quite uncomfortable after I turned down his invitation to join his weekly service, but not with Rev. Maybe getting me to agree to come to the next Easter service, the first one since I was a pre-teenager, was enough of an accomplishment for him for now. He was a few years older than me, and I'm closing in on forty. He's of average height, and his hair color is kind of salt and pepper. His wavy mop was a tad longer than you'd expect from a preacher, but this was ESVA after all, and there were a lot of unexpected things here. Rev smiled at me, then looked down at the dog.

"Nice looking pup you have there. What's his name?"

"Tank, which is short for Piankatank, like the river." At the mention of his name, the dog looked up curiously at me. "But he's not mine, I'm just watching him for Marlin and Kari Denton while they're up in Maryland at Casey and Dawn's wedding."

Our server came over, temporarily interrupting the conversation. We each ordered the house specialty, seacake sandwiches, along with draught beers.

"Not on duty, eh?" I asked.

Rev smiled. "God doesn't assign working hours."

"I meant, ordering a beer with lunch." I was a little confused and curious.

"I'm the minister of the Waterman's Church, and it's called that for a reason, Murph. Most of the congregation is made up of people who make or made their living on or around the water. I used to as well before I heard a different calling. Back then especially, I was far from being a saint. But I found a new path my friend, and I learned things like moderation and civility. I also discovered there was a big difference between outright drunkenness versus having a few drinks, and that reasoning works better than brawling.

"Murph, if I banned all the folks in my congregation who have a few beers with lunch or those that take a poke at their fellow man from time to time, my church would be pretty empty on most Sundays. There's more of a point to preaching sermons to sinners than non-sinners, not that there are many of those around if any, me included. And I already finished my sermon outline for tomorrow, so I guess you might say I'm as off-duty as I get.

"As far as for my being in a bar, well, you do your best business on Main Street, Murph. And if you haven't walked a mile or two in someone else's shoes, how can you relate to the things they're going through?"

"Yeah, I guess there's something to that."

Rev smiled, then paused before saying, "So, Casey and Dawn's wedding is today? Did you three have a falling out? I thought you and Casey were the best of pals."

Casey Shaw and Dawn McAllister are the two largest shareholders in *Mallard Cove* outside of Lindsay and me. I had worked for

Casey down in Florida for a decade and a half before moving up here to ESVA when he did.

"We are, and so are Lindsay and Dawn. But I used to be engaged to Dawn and the breakup wasn't pretty. It has taken the better part of three years for us to go back to being friends. Her father still wants me dead, so we all agreed it was best that I stay behind. I didn't want to rain on their parade and make things uncomfortable." The wedding is being held this afternoon up in Easton, Maryland, Dawn's hometown on the Eastern Shore.

Rev quickly decided that a change of subject would be a good idea right about now. "Speaking of sinners and doing business, did I see you walking down the dock a little while ago with the Mole?" I must've looked confused, and he explained, "Martin Stoneman, that former TV evangelist/entertainment guru. Now the current pitchman of so-called 'mystical water'. That, and I hear he has other 'products' almost ready to come down the pipeline. He calls this his 'outreach ministry.'" Rev looked disgusted.

"Um, I was showing someone a yacht this morning, but we have a policy about not commenting on our client list, Rev."

"Ah. So, it *was* the Mole. Which boat, er, *yacht* were you showing him?"

"Again, I can't confirm who my clients are. But let's just say that by chance I did happen to get a contract on that 112-foot Westport this morning."

Reve whistled, "Wow. I heard he pocketed a bundle when he sold that TV show, or rather his ministry did. He doesn't own anything himself you know; he'd have to pay tax on it all then. I'm guessing the yacht will go into the ministry too."

I smiled, "I couldn't comment on that, or again, who the buyer might be."

"You don't have to; I know I'm right."

It had come as a shock to me when I recognized the Mole, although I only knew him by his given name. I've heard the stories about televangelists who own private jets, or as Rev said, their *ministries* own private jets for their leader's exclusive use. Multiple houses, too, so why not yachts? One tax dodge is as good as another, and the price of the Westport was a fraction of what many of the large-bodied private jets go for these days. A lot of the dots were now starting to get connected. Stoneman sure hadn't taken a vow of poverty, or at least his ministry hadn't. The man was nobody's fool, though he might be everybody's fraud.

Rev asked, "Do you think he'll be moving it up to his new complex?"

"What're you talking about?"

"The office and production facility he built up off Magothy Bay, just past Carlton Albury's boatyard, on the grounds of the old Smithfield estate that he bought. I hear he's renovating the main house there too and has moved out of Virginia Beach permanently. He's also building homes on that property for his kids. He's become paranoid about security and takes a bodyguard around with him a lot of the time. Mostly because he can't go anywhere over in VA Beach without being recognized and accosted. And with this new scam, he's focused on, there's good reason for him to be worried.

"While he's careful not to make specific promises, he uses 'shills' in the audiences of his huge 'made for television' specials. They claim to be the recipients of large checks, job promotions, big boats, sobriety, and new homes all because they drank his so-called 'mystical water' that he wants to send them. Water that he supposedly blesses, though I've read several articles that claim it comes straight from the grocery store and gets processed without him so much as ever even seeing it. It gets repackaged in these little plastic condiment pouches like you find with fast food from a drive-thru. Then they film some of the recipients professing to have received their own miracles."

"Sounds a little cynical on your part, Rev. Don't you believe in miracles?"

"Miracles? Of course, I do, Murph. Real ones, though they're not as common as people would like 'em to be. Everybody would love a miracle, and they'd like it right now. This leaves the door open for charlatans like the Mole to make promises to the people who are so desperate to find them. Yes, I called him a charlatan, and for good reason. He airs his services on the internet and uses television ads to convince people to call in and claim their 'free' water so that they too can have a miracle in their life. Only, the people they reach on the phone are professional telemarketers and scam artists, skilled at getting information and/or money out of the callers.

"These poor folks have no idea that this 'free' water has a big catch attached. They'll now be barraged with phone calls, emails, and postal mailers. The scammers are skilled at getting people, especially lonely elderly people, to talk with them. They pick up on small bits of information that they can use to help pry money out of them. Anything positive that happens in these folk's lives they'll say happened because of the 'mystical water'. And they get urged to share their good fortune with Stoneman's ministry, which will no doubt ensure that there will be even larger blessings coming their way. And the callers are urged to use a credit card to make an offering, or they can send a check, or even jewelry if they don't have any cash. They're told that the larger the offering, the bigger the miracle."

"You've got to be kidding."

Rev shook his head, "Wish I was. It's a professional organization that has several dozen employees. This is big time."

"How do they get away with this?"

Rev shrugged. "The government is scared to death to question much of anything that's involved in a religious non-profit, much less an actual church. The IRS can only start an inquiry if a 'high-level' Treasury official has credible information to give him or her 'reasonable belief' of impropriety. The government wants nothing to do with crossing that inferred 'separation of church and state' line. By the way, the Mole calls his organization a ministry, but it's actually a church."

"Wait, what? Isn't that the same thing?"

"Not according to the IRS. Ministries operating as religious non-profits have to disclose much more financial information than churches. As a church, they are exempt from most if not all government financial reporting requirements. Things such as how much the administrators are paid and even what the church's annual income is aren't disclosed."

I was shocked that there would be so little oversight of his operation. "So, how does the public know how much money he takes in, and where it goes?"

"That's the point, Murph, they don't. For a small church like mine, it saves us from having to spend a lot of money on a CPA. The church property is all tax-exempt, but we still have to maintain the building and grounds. And then there's my salary, though it's only about the same as what I made back when I was fishing. This was never about the money for me. And after all the bills are paid, there's very little left in the church coffers. What there is we spend on the needy folks within the congregation, and within our church, there's never a shortage of them. Though for the Mole, this rule gives him a huge loophole to hide behind."

Our server brought our beers, interrupting the conversation again. For me, it was a welcome pause as I pondered what Rev had just told me. Hey, I know that not every boat owner in *Mallard Cove* is honest, and that fact isn't limited just to our marina. But after hearing the details of the story behind my latest customer, I needed a long draw off my beer to take my mind off where the money was coming from for our new yacht brokerage's biggest sale to date. Because apparently unlike the Mole, I do have a conscience.

2

SILVER KING

Rev whistled as I opened the boathouse door and turned on the lights. Floating in the single slip was a beautiful, twenty-four-foot Winter custom outboard named *Incognito*. Like all of her fiberglass-over-wood North Carolina sisterships, she has the characteristic wide bow flare that had been developed specifically to handle the mid-Atlantic sea conditions. But unlike so many of her sisterships, *Incognito* is different in her lack of teak deck and gunwale covering boards, keeping much of her maintenance to a minimum. The only teak wood in the entire boat is the varnished helm pod that contains the steering wheel, throttle, and engine instrumentation. Everything else is painted with a tough, white, polyurethane. The deck and covering boards have special rough particles added to their paint to make these surfaces non-skid. She was one serious custom-built fishing machine.

I smiled and said, "Casey lets me borrow her whenever I want to fish inshore."

I took a pair of spinning rods from their rack on the wall and carried them over to the boat, placing them in the rod holders on the back of the lean seat. Rev passed me the drink cooler as well as a five-gallon bucket of bait and ice. Then he joined me on deck, the two of us having decided to go tarpon fishing on the spur of the moment during lunch. Rather, the *three* of us, since Tank is already onboard. He had taken his place up in the bow as soon as I let him off his leash. As Rev had told me, his outline for tomorrow's sermon was already finished, and I left the brokerage office covered by one of our salesmen. So, we were both free for the rest of the afternoon.

With our stretch of unseasonably warm weather, the water temperature had remained more like what you'd expect in August, the month when the tarpon are the most prevalent on Virginia's Eastern Shore. Not that they were ever as prolific here as down in the Florida Keys. This is the farthest point north that you can find this species. It's a novelty to catch one up here at all, and we both know we have a slim chance of finding a straggler that's late in starting the long migration back south. But time spent out on the water still beats time at the dock any day. And if we do luck into one, we'll have a good story to tell.

I pressed a button on a fob attached to the ignition key, raising the boathouse's rollup door as I started the big single outboard. Rev cast off the dock lines and I maneuvered the boat out into the small basin. A handful of Casey and Dawn's friends live aboard in this private mini marina that's separate but adjacent to *Mallard Cove*. Two of the inhabitants are Lindsay and me, living on our houseboat named *On Coastal Time*. But I'll be the only one staying in this little cove tonight since all the rest are up at the wedding. They cruised up with Casey and Dawn on their 110-foot Hargrave yacht, *Lady Dawn*, two days ago. All of them but Casey and Dawn will be returning tomorrow on a chartered tour bus.

I looked to my right, past the half dozen boats and houseboats that stay here, to the large empty slip next to the bulkhead where *Lady Dawn* is normally moored. She wouldn't be back for a couple of weeks after Casey and Dawn take a New England honeymoon cruise aboard. So, I'm glad that Rev agreed to go fishing this afternoon since the cove feels strangely empty without the gang. There is almost always something going on around here, but not today, so I wasn't up for hanging around by myself.

Glancing to my left, *C2* looked like it had been abandoned. *C2* stands for the *Cove Club*, a neat little facility with a heated pool, hot tub, outdoor kitchen, and a two-story thatch-roofed Seminole Indian-built chickee. There's also a large indoor "clubhouse" with a bar, widescreen television, bathrooms, sauna, steam room, several couches, and a pool table. Off to the side is a small guest suite. Believe it or not, this had all sprung up around the pool table. Casey loves to play pool, but no matter how large your yacht is, pool tables of course aren't practical.

Casey lost the first pool table he ever owned in a divorce almost twenty years ago. Ever since that day, he's lived aboard boats, nixing any chance for a replacement. He always wanted another pool table along with a clubhouse to go with it, and *C2* was the result. This was a bigger, improved copy of one he built at the *Bayside Resort and Marina* where he used to live, and that he and Dawn still own the majority of. They moved down here a couple of months ago, though the reason for the move is a long story for another day.

I steered for the middle of the narrow inlet into the cove, looking left and right as we idled out beyond the rip-rap breakwater and into the start of the Virginia Inside Passage, which runs in front of our little marina. This portion of the Passage was dredged through the very southernmost tip of ESVA. Barely a hundred yards wide, each shore is flanked by a grassy marshland. Seeing no traffic in the channel, I steered to the left, up toward the state park that borders *C2's* northern property line. I slowly advanced the throttle, easing *Incognito* up onto a plane, allowing her to skip across the glassy flat surface of the protected section of the Passage. A little over a mile ahead the cut ended as we entered Magothy Bay, a two-mile-wide, open waterway that was bordered by the ESVA peninsula on the left, and several barrier island marshes on the right. Tank kept watch from the bow, the wind occasionally making his ears flap.

Neither of us humans said anything, even though at cruising

speed the four-stroke engine was quiet enough to permit conversation. We've both ridden in boats thousands of times over the years. Yet neither of us ever seems to tire of the feel of the hull running on top of the water, and the wind rushing past us. While maybe not as thrilling now as back when we were kids, there is still an undeniable excitement that goes along with each new boat ride. This is part of the allure that made it worth the effort to make the trip, even if our quarry decides not to cooperate today. It doesn't have so much to do with the destination, as it is about the journey itself. And the camaraderie. This beats being stuck at the dock all by myself.

A few miles north we passed a cut on the left that led back through the marsh to Carlton Albury's boatyard. We could see the buildings there, set back on the harder, drier ground. In one of those onsite buildings is ESVACats, a catamaran sailboat production company in which Lindsay and I own a minority interest. I have to give credit to Casey for that, and much more. I learned a lot back when I worked for him, the most important thing being how to spot an opportunity and act on it. Two years ago, I did that with *Mallard Cove*, when the previous owner approached Lindsay and me to buy him out. He knew we had just won the richest billfish tournament in the world and had seven figures worth of prize money on hand.

But Casey talked us into letting him and a select group of partners into the deal, and I'm glad he did. The folks he put together made financing the needed improvements and subsequent expansions a cinch. Without him, Lindsay and I would've run out of cash after only patching up the docks and upgrading the fuel pumps. Then Casey and Dawn let us invest in a few more deals with them, spreading out our risk and giving us a nice cash flow. It beats the heck out of having to charter my sixty-foot Merritt sport fisherman just for Lindsay and me to scrape out a living. To put it mildly, Casey has been a great friend to both of us.

REV AND I ran along the west side of the bay because I wanted to fish a small but deep spur off that side of Magothy Channel, which links

Magothy Bay with Mockhorn Bay, just to the north. The spur channel cuts back through the marsh and land by Dunton Cove, which the old Smithfield place borders, now apparently the new home of the Mole.

Rev asked, "You heading for the little channel?"

I nodded. "Spud told me he saw some bait moving through there the other day, and something was chasing them that left a trail of bubbles."

Tarpon are known to sometimes leave a bubble trail. And Timmy "Spud" O'Shea was a pal who owned Spud's Trolling Baits, which occupies the other side of the building that also contains our yacht brokerage office. His baits are famous, and in high demand not just around the mid-Atlantic, but up and down the east coast and the Caribbean too. Spud knows his bait, and what chases them as well. This is why I bought some large greenies from him before we left and now had them in a mixture of ice and brine in the bucket.

Rev said, "Then you'll get a good look at the Mole's new place. He's right on Dunton Cove, overlooking that channel."

"Yeah, I know that place. Nice digs. Just didn't realize it had been sold."

I changed course a little more to the east to clear the group of marsh islands that stick out into the bay, forming the south side of the cove. As we cleared the point I throttled back, letting the hull settle down into the water while switching from planing to displacement. We needed to approach slowly, so as not to spook any tarpon that might be in the area.

"See? I told you he was moving his operation," Rev said.

I looked over at the old Smithfield place a quarter mile away and was surprised to see a long, new dock extending out from the shore into the muddy marsh. It had a boat lift on the north side that was occupied by a large center console boat with twin outboards. And up next to the three-story main house, two other large houses were in the process of being built. Each would have an equally stunning view of both the cove and the bay.

But the biggest surprise was an enormous metal building that was almost out of sight of the houses, set far back from the water to the south. It looked like a large farm barn. But from what Rev had said earlier, I knew this was the new home of the Mole's "outreach ministry" business. Though I'm having a hard time calling it a ministry.

"Wow, I haven't been up this way in a while. He's gotten a lot done since then," I said.

Rev replied, "You know how fast those metal buildings go up. And you get a lot done when you're willing to pay builders overtime to work weekends."

That's when I noticed that both of the new houses had framing crews still working around them. Not something you often see around here on a Saturday afternoon this close to deer season.

"I guess he was in a hurry to get out of VA Beach."

"He's living here in the main house, with his adult children, but he wants to get his kids moved into those other houses," Rev said.

"You sure know an awful lot about him," I commented.

"He got all chatty with me when he tried to buy my church."

"He did what?" I exclaimed. "How do you go about buying a church?"

"By talking the vestry into it. Technically, the church property belongs to the congregation, and it's managed by the vestry, whose members are elected by the congregation to run it. They hired me, and they oversee the maintenance of the building and grounds, as well as set our church's goals and objectives.

"A few years before I got hired, the vestry had let the place go. It wasn't their fault, the tough economy back then meant they didn't have the money to fix it up. So, they ended up taking out a big loan and getting us much farther into debt than they should've. When I became the minister, I talked them into making reducing that debt our number one priority. While we could've survived if we had lost the building because the 'church' is made up of people, not wood and nails. But if new families have the choice between joining a church that has a building or one that meets in a tent..." His voice trailed off.

I said, "I get it. So, the Mole smelled blood in the water, and he came calling."

"Yeah, as I told you, he wanted to go from being a ministry to a church, and to do that the IRS wants to see something in brick and mortar. But what the Mole didn't know was that the Scott family had been going to our church for generations, and the last of their line had just passed away. She left the church enough money to pay off all our debts and create a small endowment for the future.

"Boy, was the Mole ever torqued over that. He figured he had us squeezed and could replace our vestry with his people. After his plan fell through, he ended up buying an old, abandoned church up the road a bit from us, and he's dumping a bunch of money in it to make it habitable." Rev grinned at the memory.

"So, what's he going to do for a congregation," I asked.

"His employees. They're required to belong. It's not legal of course, but a lot of what he does either isn't or shouldn't be."

Both of us went silent, and I kept looking over at the property and the dock. "Well, there's no way he's going to get that Westport in there." The dock was surrounded by mudflats, and a shallow, narrow channel had been cut from the deep water of the bay back to it. A small turning basin in front of the dock looked barely large enough for a decent-sized outboard to use.

Rev nodded. "Looks like you'll keep him as a customer. There's no marina between here and *Mallard Cove* that can accommodate that yacht."

"Not my first choice for a customer, but hey, dockage is dockage." It bothered me though, now that I knew where the money was coming from.

We both turned from that shore, changing our focus to the bluish-brown water in front of us as we crept up on the mouth of the spur channel. Without even the hint of a breeze, it was easy to read the water. I could see a slight current caused by the tide, and an upwelling from what I suspected was a large hole. It was a perfect spot for tarpon to lay as they waited to ambush bait moving with the tide. If there were any still around, chances were that this is the place they'd be. I didn't spot any tarpon rolling on the surface, nor any tell-tale bubbles that might indicate one was "home." But that didn't always happen where there's enough current, especially when they're lying in wait for their prey.

Rev hooked up the head of a greenie that he had cut in half. Tarpon are opportunistic feeders. They'll hit live bait, and also will feed on fresh dead bait, too. But these cunning fish can be wary, so by cutting the bait in half, it made it look like the remainder of a fresh kill by a toothy predator.

I eased us up to within casting range of that hole. Rev and Tank swapped places, with Tank coming back to stand next to me. Then Rev made a perfect cast, overshooting the hole by ten feet. He slowly retrieved the bait as I held *Incognito* in position. As he reeled in, the half a greenie made its way down into the hole like it was drifting with the current. Rev eased it along until it appeared to snag on something. Since we were using circle hooks, Rev continued reeling. You don't "set the hook" with a circle hook, you just keep reeling until it comes tight, wedging itself in the corner of the fish's mouth. These hooks are designed to make it much easier to release the fish unharmed, without "gut hooking" them, which is frequently fatal. Suddenly line started peeling off the spool, and the water erupted. A tarpon that was well over a hundred pounds leaped out of the water, twisting and gyrating in midair.

"Bow, Rev, bow!" He was new to tarpon fishing and wasn't used to giving fish slack once they were hooked. But tarpon, also known as Silver Kings, are a different animal. Keep too much tension on the line when they break the surface, and you'll end up with nothing. Their wild antics will snap the line every time. I had "schooled" Rev about this, but it still went against every fisherman's instinct. This inspired the saying, *"Bow to the Silver King"* to remind new tarpon anglers how to react.

Fortunately, Rev understood. He bowed and extended his rod arm forward, giving the awesome fish the slack necessary to keep from breaking the line. Then the tarpon took off like a freight train, and the chase was on. Tank started barking, seeming as if he wanted to encourage Rev. Then the tarpon passed us headed south, and I turned our bow to give chase. Rev handled the rod like the pro that he is. I could see by the look on his face that he was having the time of his life, engaged in one of the greatest fish fights of his life. I kept up with the tarpon for the next half hour as we endured its heart-stopping aerobatics, knowing that any of these leaps could be the last that we'd see of this magnificent fish.

I wasn't the only spectator. As the fish turned us toward the shore, I saw a lone figure out on the dock at the Mole's; it was the man himself. The fish was making his way toward that dock's channel, giving him quite a show. Then seemingly out of nowhere came a huge, forty-something-foot, half-million-dollar-plus center console with three giant outboard engines that was headed way too close to us.

The middle-aged dumbass at the helm was aiming for the Mole's channel, despite us having a leaping fish right in his path. I was screaming and cursing at him as I tried to wave him off. As he passed, the moron was undoubtedly close enough to hear everything I yelled, but he completely ignored me, focused solely on heading up the Mole's channel. Thankfully, just before this idiot was about to run over our line, the fish turned just enough to avoid his boat. That's when I spotted the name on the side, *Rev'd Up*. His wake slammed us broadside, rocking us violently. Somehow all three of us managed to keep our footing and Rev also kept his fish. After we finish catching this tarpon, I intend on catching up with this idiot and giving him a lesson in courtesy on the water.

Finally, the tarpon was tiring, and Rev was gaining line. The leaps were now few and far between, and five minutes later we had the fish at the side of the boat. It took both of us to lift this monster over the gunwale and onto the deck for pictures, hook removal, and measurements. Fifty-three inches, and well over a hundred pounds. Then we gently put the fish back in the water, with Rev holding it by its toothless jaw as I idled the boat slowly forward, forcing water through its gills. It quickly regained its strength, and with a firm shake of its head, it was gone.

While you normally wouldn't haul a fish you plan on releasing into your boat because they can't breathe out of the water, tarpon are a different breed. After millions of years of evolution, they have developed a swim bladder that also acts as a lung, allowing them to breathe while out of the water. They take in gulps of air when they roll, which is why they leave a bubble trail, they're exhaling. It's also one of the reasons they're such great fighters since they're able to take in more oxygen during their acrobatic leaps. Without a doubt, they're one of my favorite gamefish.

Rev reached into the cooler, bypassing the bottles of water and removing two beers, handing one to me. I shut down the engine, and we drifted in near silence as we both savored and celebrated the moment after the catch.

"That was my first tarpon," he said. "Lived here all my life but never caught one. Heck, never even seen one that I can remember. Was it citation size?"

"By over seventeen inches," I replied. "And not many people were targeting them around here until the last couple of decades from what I've heard."

"Well, I will be from now on. Murph, that was one of, if not *the* best fish fights of my life. Thank you."

I smiled, "Thank your 'boss,' I was only the guide."

"Oh, believe me, I'll thank Him as well. Moments like this are probably one of the reasons He put us here."

I figure that Rev is more of an expert on such things than me, so I didn't need to weigh in. Not that I don't believe in a God, or a Higher Power, I'm just not that well versed in religion. I did know this, I trusted Rev's opinion on these matters much more than that of my latest brokerage customer.

Speaking of my latest customer, I was suddenly aware of angry voices traveling over the water, and one of them was the Mole's. I looked over toward his dock now a little over two hundred yards away, and saw *Rev'd Up* was tied up at the end. The jerk who had waked us and almost cost us a Virginia citation-sized fish was on the dock, in a heated argument with the Mole. At the rate it was going, it didn't sound like it would last much longer. They'd probably either come to blows, or one of them would leave before it went that far. I didn't care which scenario came to be, so long as it happened quickly. That guy on the boat and I are due for a chat.

3

DREDGING FOR OYSTERS

As it turned out, I didn't have long to wait. As I suspected, the argument on the dock was soon over and ended with the Mole stomping off. Neither Rev nor I could make out what had been said during the confrontation, but I didn't care. I started the engine and moved *Incognito* up across the Mole's narrow channel just inside the mouth, blocking the jerk's only exit. We watched as he climbed aboard *Rev'd Up* and cast off, backing into the side of the Mole's turning basin, stirring up a cloud of mud in the process. Then he got into the throttles, trying to spin the boat on its axis by putting the gears of two outside engines in opposing directions and giving them plenty of gas. The excess throttle bit is a classic "newbie" move and usually doesn't end well. This time was no exception, with the guy at the helm quickly jamming the one engine from reverse into forward then oversteering as he tried to keep away from the basin's shallow edge. It didn't work, as the stern of the boat was now pushed sideways into the bank again.

I'll give him this, the deep part of the basin was at best marginal for a boat of his size. The Mole's boat up on the lift was probably ten to fifteen feet shorter, and better suited to the place. But this guy was clearly in over his head here. It's at the dock or the boat ramp where you can more easily spot "newbie" boaters. And while Virginia does require an operator's license to run a boat of this size, you can get one at home, sitting at a computer, without ever having to set foot aboard. Try that with a car or an airplane license; it's not happening. I'm willing to bet this guy hasn't spent much time on the water. That he has more money than sense was obvious.

He finally managed to get his boat centered up in the channel, and that's when he spotted us and realized there was no way for him to get by. So, what does he do? Adds throttle up to a high idle so that he could back down dramatically when he reached us. Another newbie move, the nautical equivalent of puffing out your chest.

From his helm, he yelled, "Hey! Move your boat, you're blocking my way." He sounded every bit as obnoxious as he acted.

I smiled and yelled back, "Funny you should say that since you almost cut off our fish and then rocked the hell out of us when you pulled in here. You know, courtesy on the water goes both ways."

"Don't you curse at me! I left you plenty of room, and you were blocking this channel then too, just like you are now. Either move your boat, or I'll move it for you!" He was still amped up from his argument with the Mole, and his trouble trying to get the boat turned around.

"I would've thought that as a reverend you would have better manners and attitude than that," Rev said.

The man on the other boat seemed surprised then squinted as he looked at Rev like he was trying to recall where he might have met him. "Who're you?"

"Just another preacher of the gospel. But one who believes in treating his fellow man kindly, and with respect."

"In that case, you'll back out of my way and let me pass."

Rev sighed, "I might if I was running this boat, but I'm not. And I do think my friend would like an apology first."

Instead of apologizing, the man spun the wheel on his helm and pushed his throttles forward. His bow hit *Incognito*'s stainless steel rub rail just forward of her transom. With him again increasing his speed, it shoved our stern sideways. But only a boating newbie wouldn't have anticipated what came next as his bow rebounded off us, turning him toward the edge of the channel. Only this time his props found not just soft mud on this bank, but an oyster bar, instantly bending the blade tips on two of them.

He might have been able to react a bit sooner and avoid the damage if he hadn't been so preoccupied. As he passed where I was standing, I slung the entire contents of our bait bucket at him, scoring a direct hit with the icy, fishy contents. His polo-style shirt and khaki shorts were now soaked in freezing brine, and greenies covered the deck at his feet. He was shocked, sputtering, and concentrating on the front of his clothes at first, then he turned and vented his anger on me with language I'm sure he didn't learn in any theology class.

Suddenly it dawned on him that he could feel a wicked vibration through his feet, and he figured out what it was. Again, I don't get why newbies think the answer to most situations is to add more throttle. In his case, the proper action would have been to shift into neutral and tilt the engines up until they were no longer hitting bottom. Then he should've slowly and carefully backed out until he was in the clear. But with 1,350 horsepower hanging off his transom, I guess this guy felt he could power his way through anything. The large rock that was mixed in with the oysters proved it otherwise as the starboard prop lost a blade and the rest were badly mangled.

While he was busy tearing things up, I checked the edge of our covering board and its stainless rub rail, which luckily for his sake wasn't even scratched. I couldn't say the same for the bow paint on *Rev'd Up*, which now had a three-foot-long scratch. The guy running her had finally wised up and shut down the engines and was in the process of raising them to assess the damage. Even from my vantage point about twenty feet away, I could see his props as they broke the surface, and two were toast. He looked from them over to me and started yelling about a lawsuit.

"If anybody is going to sue, that would be me, for you ramming us and nearly swamping us earlier," I yelled.

"You assaulted me! I'll have you arrested!"

I laughed, "On what charge? Assault with a deadly baitfish? Just be glad you didn't hurt my friend's boat, or I'd have been the one pressing charges for reckless boating! Hang on, Rev, we're outta here."

Normally I'd have never left without rendering assistance to another boater in trouble out on the water, but this jerk could just figure it out on his own. I backed away from the edge of the channel and briefly flirted with the idea of raising my engine almost out of the water and goosing it, throwing a firehose volume of prop wash into the cockpit of the other boat. But I'd already extracted enough payment out of this guy with my bait bucket, and I figured we were close to even.

"If I see you out on the water again, I'll run you over!" The guy just didn't know when to leave well enough alone. Fortunately for him, by that time I'd already turned us far enough away so that he was no longer in prop wash range.

Rev moved back and stood next to me as Tank returned to his place at the bow. I idled us out and turned south.

Rev looked at me and asked, "Aren't you going to take a shot at a tarpon?"

I shook my head. "All our bait is back in that other boat, and I don't think I want to go ask for it back." I laughed. "Besides, my goal was to get you your first tarpon. Mission accomplished."

"I guess that's probably a good idea. Keller looked pretty torqued off."

"Who?"

"The Reverend Joseph Keller. You know, the guy who recently laid out big bucks for the Mole's old TV show. He moved to Virginia Beach this year to run it."

I snorted, "He sounded more like a studio boss than a preacher. And it looks like the first thing he did when he arrived was buy that boat."

"You're probably not too far off in either case, except I doubt that boat is in his name. Probably belongs to the production company."

I asked, "Which is in turn owned by the ministry?"

"Church. Keller doesn't miss a tax trick, either."

"How could he justify an almost seven-figure outboard..."

Rev shrugged, "If you want the best guests on that TV show, you need to be able to entertain them when they get here. It doesn't matter that the show is focused on religion. Hey, the Mole's whole complex is owned by his new church. The old Smithfield manor house is the parsonage, and the kids' houses are part of it. Guest quarters, all covered under the veil of the church's tax exemption."

"Unbelievable. So why don't you have more in the way of frills, Rev?"

"I don't need much, Murph, and my congregation is far from wealthy. Asking them to give more than they can afford so that I can live better isn't what I believe in. The Mole is the one that preaches the prosperity gospel, not me. I'm more interested in seeing that the members of my congregation all have good lives. And that they chose to help others however they can, not so that they will be enriched monetarily, but because it's what we are supposed to do as Christians. Sometimes that's volunteering at the food bank, having a bake sale, or holding a spaghetti dinner to help someone pay unexpected medical bills.

"As for me, I have our own parsonage's roof over my head, and food on my table. I'm comfortable. And I just got to fight one of the finest creatures our Creator ever put in the ocean. How could I ask for more than that?"

"Your church can afford a parsonage?"

"Well, it's not exactly like the Mole's. It's an older trailer behind the church building. But it's warm in the winter and cool in the summer, and the roof doesn't leak. A few in my congregation aren't quite as fortunate, and truthfully I feel a bit guilty about that."

I nodded slowly. There was a lot of comfort in what he said, and how he saw his congregation as his responsibility, not solely as his income source. But much of what I learned today about the Mole and his cohorts bothered me, so it was reassuring to know there were still some leaders of the faithful that don't treat their churches like personal ATMs. Hopefully, the others like the Mole and Keller are few and far between. Rev was indeed the "real deal," and I looked forward to doing a lot more fishing as well as hanging out with him in the future.

BACK AT THE BOATHOUSE, after we washed down both the gear and the boat, Rev took off. I thought it was probably because he had a sermon to give in the morning, but he said no, it was because he had a date tonight. I never really thought about preachers dating, but then again, I hadn't thought about them having beers with lunch or when they went fishing, either. And I knew that in some denominations they couldn't or wouldn't. To be honest, I'd never even given the life of a preacher much thought before. I guess you have the Mole and Keller on one end, living the life of multi-millionaires, and those like Rev on the other end, and a lot that falls somewhere in between. Rev didn't seem anything like the preachers you see on TV, but more like a close friend who happens to give good spiritual advice. I get the feeling his congregation is more like a large extended family, and that they look up to him as they would a wise and compassionate uncle. I know this, they're darn lucky to have him.

It was already late afternoon, and in the distance, I was catching strains of music from the *Driftwood Stage* we built on the sand behind the *Beach Bar* last year. I briefly considered heading over there to listen. But with Lindsay out of town, and me "flying solo" until she got back, I didn't need to look like I was out "trolling" while she was gone. That's when I realized the song that was playing in the distance was that old Sam Cooke tune, *Another Saturday Night*. Yeah, and I wasn't about to live out those lyrics about a lonely guy out looking to meet women.

I'd had a well-earned reputation as a "player" back a few years ago down in Palm Beach, but that was long before I met Lindsay. Then I'd been engaged to Dawn when Lindsay and I met, which you'll recall is why I'm not up at Casey's wedding. Before you think badly of Linds, I hadn't told her about Dawn. And that's another of those stories for some other time, though you get the drift. But something changed in me when I met Lindsay, and it was for the better.

I looked down at the dog, "Tank, how about you and I go over to C2 and have a beer or two by ourselves." He looked up at me and wagged his tail. I'd love to know what he thought I said. Or maybe he did understand English, who knows? In any case, he was my drinking partner this afternoon, though he'd have to settle for water. We climbed the small hill to the patio. It was several feet higher than the surrounding field since this is where they spread the fill from when they dug the pool and dredged the silt out of the boat basin. The extra height made for a nice view of the Passage out past the jetty, as well as the boats in the little cove. I grabbed a beer and then sat on a chaise while Tank lay down next to me.

I no sooner had gotten comfortable before I saw *Rev'd Up* coming down the channel. He wasn't making a lot of speed, just barely above idle. His starboard engine was tilted up, and he wasn't pushing hard. With that center prop as dinged as it was, there was little doubt that this was as fast as Keller could go without doing some real damage to that lower unit's shaft seal and bearings. But if he was from VA Beach like Rev said, I wonder why he didn't take the more direct route around Skidmore Island and straight across to home? The Passage would dump him out behind Fisherman Island, adding a few extra miles to his trip.

I was still pondering this when I had an incoming video call. Lindsay. I saw that her makeup and hair were all done up for the wedding – she was the Maid of Honor – and she looked like a million bucks. "Hey, Linds."

"Hey, Babe! How're you getting along there without me?"

"Oh, Tank and I are being a pair of real party animals." I put my beer down on the ground next to Tank, then pointed the camera at him. As if on cue he started wagging his tail.

"Aw, you guys are hanging by yourselves at C2? Tank looks lonely. There's supposed to be music tonight at the *Driftwood Stage*, why don't you guys go over there and listen?"

"I didn't want to go without you or at least with some of the gang. And everybody is up there with you."

"We'll all be back early tomorrow. There's a brunch for everybody in the morning, then the tour bus ride home. We should get there a little after noon. I miss you."

"Yeah, me too. Got an interesting story about Rev and me, but I'll wait until you're home to tell it."

Suddenly her video started spinning around and I was looking at the face of Captain Bill "Baloney" Cooper. "Murph! Yer missin' one helluva party!"

"And you're missing a cigar!"

"Yeah, well, Betty hid the damn things, scared I was gonna light up at the reception."

I laughed, "Smart move, I can't blame her. The third day, you've got to be going into withdrawals."

"Uh, well, I did manage to sneak and light up a couple before she hid 'em. But never mind that – I'm here to collect your gal for a dance."

The video switched back to a laughing Lindsay. "I'm getting swept off my feet, so I better go."

"That would be quite a sight. Okay, you have fun."

"You, too! But you and Tank go enjoy the music, and I'll see you tomorrow. Love you! Eek!" Right before the screen went blank, I could see she was being yanked toward a dance floor.

The mental image in my mind of that dance floor made me chuckle. At five-foot-six inches, Lindsay and Baloney were about the same height. But he was almost thirty years older than her, balding with gray sides. And Fred Astaire he's not. But he enjoys life more than just about anyone I know yet he gripes about it nearly as much.

Baloney and his wife Betty have been married about the same number of years that Lindsay's been alive. I don't know anyone else who would've put up with him that long or adored him half as much as Betty does. And he adores her as much or more, even letting her put strict rules on his cigar intake. The truth was, she was saving the sense of smell for the rest of us at the docks. He's not supposed to light one up until after he passes the marina breakwater, though he normally has an unlit one in his mouth at all times back on shore.

The "sticks" that Baloney prefers are the cheapest ones around.

They're more noxious than the exhaust of his old forty-eight-foot wooden charter boat, the *Golden Dolphin*, that he ran up until last year. That's when he turned it over to his mate Bobby to run it for him. Like Baloney, the *Dolphin* was originally from New Jersey. He now runs a fifty-four-foot Viking named *My Mahi*. It was also made in New Jersey, but he bought this one when it was literally underwater. Two salvaged engines, new wiring, and a new interior later, and he had both a new home and ride.

He finished *Mahi* just in time to use it to become the biggest star on the *Tuna Hunters* reality show that's owned by Marlin and Kari Denton's fishing foundation. Over the past year, Baloney has gone from barely scraping by to bringing in just over seven figures. You'd think he'd spring for better stogies, but that wasn't happening.

Yeah, you'd never know that Baloney was rapidly becoming a wealthy guy. He's still the largest and most unapologetic beer mooch on the docks, coming in right behind Sanford "Sandy" Morgan, the bestselling author, who lives aboard his trawler, *Epilogue*, in the small cove during the warmer months. Sandy was also up at the wedding this weekend, and I pitied the bartenders with both him and Baloney being in the same crowd.

I looked down at Tank, "Well, big guy, we just got our marching orders. I hope you're a music fan." Again, he looked up and started wagging his tail. I clipped the leash to his collar, and we walked next door to *Mallard Cove*. We could've taken my golf cart since it was a bit of a hike past all the docks over there, but I figured we could both do with the exercise.

I'm glad I chose to walk instead of ride, or I might not have noticed *Rev'd Up* occupying one of the transient slips. All three of her engines were tilted up, and even from over on the bulkhead, I could easily see two of the props were trashed. That explained the mystery of why Keller had come down the Passage. *Mallard Cove* was the closest marina between the Mole's and VA Beach. With his props so badly damaged, it would've taken a couple of hours or more for him to cross the open-water mouth of the Chesapeake. He probably plans to put new props on here. Or rather, he probably plans to have it done for him.

I say that because I saw that he has one of the dock kids cleaning his rig. These are teenagers that hang around picking up mate and washdown jobs in the summer and after school. I used to be one myself down in Palm Beach Shores, Florida many years ago. This kid was picking up all the bait that I'd thrown on Keller, who despite a long, slow ride down here must've found it beneath him to toss the greenies over the side on the way. What a tool.

Tank and I rounded the far corner of the long dock, turning onto Charter Boat Row, walking behind those first two boats that comprise Baloney's *Dolphin Fleet*. He even sells tee shirts with the fleet name printed on them. He's become quite the entrepreneur, capitalizing on all his newfound fame. He and the rest of the *Tuna Hunters* cast bring in a lot of curious tourists that end up having lunch and drinks. So, good business for him means good business for us as well.

We built a large, covered patio onto our *Mallard Cove Restaurant* that overlooks all of the fishing cockpits of the charter boats. I've been eating here on more than one occasion when I've heard groups decide to book charters after seeing the boats unload nice catches. It works well for all of us.

Tank and I were only halfway down the dock when I heard an angry voice yelling from the patio, "You!"

I looked over and saw a very red-faced Joseph Keller standing up at his table and pointing at me. Then he started toward the stairs that led down to the dock. Tank and I stopped and stood our ground, only about ten feet away from the base of the stairs. Keller charged down at me, still yelling. Mimi Carter, the general manager of our restaurants and bars, had been going from table to table talking with customers on the patio and had heard the commotion. She also made for the stairs, not far behind Keller.

Keller charged up to me, wagging a finger in front of my face, and drawing a low growl from Tank.

"You owe me for two propellers and a mechanics bill!"

I smiled, making him even angrier. "In your dreams, pal."

He sputtered and was about to start yelling again when Mimi stepped in between Keller and me.

"Sir, please lower your voice, you're disturbing the other diners." A few curious onlookers had started gathering behind us on the dock.

Without lowering his voice, Keller demanded, "Who are you!"

"I'm the manager here, and you need to calm down and go back to your table."

"Not until I'm finished with this guy!"

"Sir, either go back to your table now, or I'm going to have to ask you to leave."

"*Me*? What about *him*!"

"He isn't causing the issue here. And besides that, I can't ask him to leave since he owns *Mallard Cove*."

The look on Keller's face was priceless, having gone from what he no doubt considered a winning hand to losing any leverage he thought he had. I noted a couple of phone cameras pointing at us, undoubtedly in video mode. I said quietly enough that only the three of us could hear it, "And Keller, I'd be happy to point these shutterbugs in the direction of the biggest TV gossip outlets after I tell them who you are. That ought to do a bit to drop your show's ratings, with its 'irreverent reverend' owner not exactly following his show's teachings. I might even tune in to watch your on-air apology. So, it's that, or you can go back to your table right now and shut up. Your choice."

His face flushed right before he silently turned on his heel and stomped his way back over and up the stairs.

"Thanks, 'Meems'. That one is a first-class jerk. I'm willing to bet he stiffs the wait staff. Check with his server when he leaves; I helped put him in a bad mood, and I don't want them to suffer for it. Make sure they get tipped well, and if they don't, give them twenty-five percent of the bill and put it on the house account."

"Got it, Murph. You and Tank headed over to the *Cove Beach Bar* by yourselves?"

"The *Catamaran*. A less rowdy crowd and not as close to the band's speakers. The gang's all up at the wedding, and I didn't feel like cooking just for one."

"You guys want some company? I'm just going to check a few things and then I'm off. I was planning on listening to the band."

"Absolutely, and dinner's on Tank and me. We'll see you over there."

4

BACHIN' IT

With the sun dipping lower in the sky, the evening's drinking crowd had started funneling into the *Beach Bar*. The *Catamaran* was a mirror image, size-wise, set across the covered breezeway that runs between them. Because the "*Cat*" was only starting to catch its evening crowd, I was able to get a good table just as the band went on break. My spot overlooked the beach and the water, and out between Smith and Fisherman Islands to the Atlantic Ocean beyond. Our *Driftwood Stage* and its beach sand dance floor were over in front of the *Beach Bar* to the right. My fleet of rental ESVACat catamaran sailboats was to my left, already pulled up high on the beach for the night by the staff.

The *Catamaran* is a fun bar and grill, but with more of a kicked-back atmosphere than the *Beach Bar,* which tends to draw the historically rowdier sportfishing folks. We decorated this bar with the more "chill" sailing and cruising crowd in mind. There were sails up on the ceiling, and the two benches up at the bar were a pair of inverted hulls from an earlier ESVACat design. The place gives off a much more serene vibe.

Baloney hates it when he has to mooch beer off me here, he calls the place "a friggin' blow-boater bar." He claims that if he's spotted in here it'll damage his reputation. And yet somehow, he always seems to show up when any of our crowd is in here and running a tab that he can add to.

Mimi arrived just as our server had delivered a paper plate of ice cubes for Tank, and a Chuck's Martini on the rocks for me. It's made with vodka from a distillery over in Cape Charles. This is dangerous stuff; when chilled it tastes like water, but it packs a real prizefighter's punch. Mimi opted for wine, a better choice for her than what I was having since she had to drive home later.

Technically, Mimi doesn't work directly for me, she's an employee of the restaurant management company which is mostly owned by Casey, Dawn, and some minority partners. Another group of partners headed by Lindsay and me own the bars and restaurants here, and we pay the management company to operate them. It's a formula that works out for all of us, and it also means that Mimi and I are friends first, as well as business associates. And now that she was "off the clock" she had put her "friend hat" on. I was still glad that we did have the business connection since she's a very attractive strawberry blonde in her mid-thirties. Our having dinner with Lindsay being out of town could've easily started rumors if we didn't quasi-work together.

"What the hell did you do to piss that guy off so badly, Murph?" Over time, she's learned that she can be blunt with me, which is her preferred way of communicating, except with customers. It doesn't bother me a bit, and I prefer it when she is. There are no games, she's straight up. Oh, and she's also forgotten more about the restaurant and bar business than most owners will ever know. I'm glad she's here.

I told her the story of my encounter with Keller, after first talking about my dealings with the Mole. While I had been hesitant to share too many business details with Rev, my business relationship with Mimi allowed for it. After I related everything, she looked as disgusted as I felt.

"So, this whole church thing is just a tax dodge for a pair of scam artists?"

"You know what they say about not judging unless you want to be judged, Meems. But if I had to guess, from what I've seen of Keller, he seems a lot more like a businessman than a preacher. He probably stumbled across the tax exemption information and decided to build a business around it.

"Think about Marlin's foundation, and all the paperwork they have to file every year just to keep their charitable status. Every dollar has to be accounted for, and every expenditure must be defensible. One screwup and they would have a huge back tax bill. Look at this guy's 'church' instead of being a charitable organization but as his own private company. It has no income or expense reporting requirements, and it can't be audited without some IRS higher-up having a darn good reason. It's a license to steal.

"I'll say this much for the Mole, he wouldn't even start our meeting without saying a prayer. While it wasn't the most sincere prayer I've ever heard, at least he went through the motions. He may well have been for real when he was younger, but as far as I'm concerned, and from what Rev said, this guy is now the lowest of the low. He's scamming the people that can least afford it and buying a yacht and an estate with the proceeds. So, I'd put them both on the same level.

"You know, ethically, I'm required to do my best to represent the seller of the yacht and get him a deal with a price he can agree to. I've done that. But I'd love to tell the Mole to shove it and get him to bugger off. After we signed the contract, I felt like I needed to take a shower to scrub all the creepiness off of me. And that was even before I found out what Rev told me about him."

She asked, "You think he'll still keep the boat here?"

I nodded. "Unfortunately. And unless he breaks the rules, we really can't kick him out. As you know, he's not the only creep we have in here, but fortunately, we don't have too many of them. And I doubt the Mole will be throwing a lot of parties. He's going to rename the yacht, '*Privacy*,' so it sounds like he wants to keep a low profile. It works for me; the guy is a bit of a buzz-kill if you know what I mean."

She laughed, "His nickname suits him well. I keep seeing his ads on television, and when he uses that tagline about wanting to give me something for free, I can't help but think it's the plague. I'd no more drink anything in those packets he gives out than I'd swig swamp water." She shuddered.

"Yeah, it makes you wonder about how sanitary his facility is, Meems. Anyway, I'm not planning on drinking any of it, either."

The band was now getting started again, and Mimi turned her chair to face the beach. She looked back over her shoulder at me and surprised me by saying, "To heck with those two, Murph. As for me, I can't ask for a better night. Good band, good drinks, and good company." She raised her glass, and I raised mine back at her. Mimi is one of those people like Rev that can make anyone feel at ease, just like she was doing now. Glad I took the walk over here.

THE DINING ROOM in the old Smithfield house was all glass at one end, with a view out over the slowly darkening marsh and Magothy Bay beyond. His two adult children were flanking him on either side of the huge table. The Mole sat at the head, farthest from the glass, facing the water. He had a faraway look as he told the story.

"It was a huge fish, leaping and gyrating like the wild animal that it was. I had no idea that tarpon lived this far north, and that we could find them literally in our backyard. Wondrous. Truly wondrous. And quite a coincidence that the broker who sold me the yacht this morning was captaining the boat that would catch it. I'm going to talk to him about taking me tarpon fishing. I'd love to have one mounted in the living room across from the windows."

Marty was disgusted, "You would kill one of God's creatures just for your own ego?"

The Mole scowled, "No, they don't kill them anymore, they release them. The mounts are made out of fiberglass from an existing mold, they don't use any part of the fish. They just take measurements and match them up to the mold."

"You could go ahead and order one, a nice one, and maybe you'll have caught yours before the mount is even finished and delivered since I hear it takes a while to make," Sandra suggested. "Even if you haven't, you can still put the mount up on the wall."

The Mole shook his head, "No, that would be bearing false witness over a fish, and I won't do that."

"Only if you claim it is anything other than decoration, father. After you catch one, you can add a photograph of you with it on the mantle, and that will give it the pedigree to prove it was that fish, without actually having made the claim. No one will know exactly when it happened. It's not lying if eventually, you can back up what people have already taken for granted."

The Mole smiled at his daughter, then looked at his son. "She has such a quick and sharp mind. You could learn so much from her."

His son bristled, "I'm the one who has the 'gift,' not Sandra. I can talk to the people just like you. They'll follow me as well."

His father shook his head sadly. "There's so much more to it than just getting people to follow you. And make no mistake, they would follow Sandra too. Knowing where to lead them, that's the other part of the equation that she understands, but you have yet to learn. Then again, that too may be a talent; something that you are given, and which can't be learned. Don't make the mistake of underestimating that part."

"If you thought Sandra was more talented than me, you'd have made her the next in line."

The Mole sighed, not ready to have this conversation yet, but also not willing to back down. "I do not doubt that at some point during your lives female ministers will be as equally and completely accepted as males, but despite the few standouts that are preaching now, sadly, we aren't quite there yet. When we are, your sister will be the biggest asset to our church. You need to understand, accept and embrace that. So far, you have been the winner of the chromosome lottery, but it won't always be that way. You'll need to prepare and be ready when that day comes because I feel like it's not that far away.

"You've brought up a good point. We need to get Sandra to step out of the background and become more visible now, both at our live events and in the commercials. We'll start this week when we film the spots for the new prayer cube. I'm going to have both of you in those with me."

Marty's face became a stormy mask as he shoved his chair back and stood up. He glared at his father, "I'm not hungry anymore, I've lost my appetite."

The Mole replied, "Martin, sit down. We haven't finished our discussion."

"Maybe you haven't, but I have." With a passing glare at his sister, Marty left the room.

The Mole sighed. "I had planned to have this talk with you two at some point later, Sandra, and I wasn't wanting to discuss it yet. But with the new spots being filmed, maybe Marty did me a favor by moving up the schedule."

Sandra grimaced slightly, knowing that her father didn't like being pushed into anything by anyone, let alone by one of his children. She decided her best course of action was to stay silent for now, even though she disagreed with him about the acceptance of women in ministry. She believed it was something that was already happening.

The Mole had been watching her closely to see what her reaction would be. He could see her mulling over the situation and could tell when she reached her conclusion. It pleased him to see that she appeared to be in silent agreement on the subject.

"We'll not only work the both of you into the spots of the prayer cube, but I want you beside me at the live events, instead of out working in the audience. You know, Marty may have done us both a favor. I was willing to wait until the world was ready to come around to equality in preaching, but maybe pushing it is something the Lord wants me to do."

Sandra smiled in both agreement and appreciation, but less in belief. Her father may always want to maintain some semblance of a religious façade, but she was a realist, preferring to look more at the business behind it. Even though she could deliver a sermon with the best and most seasoned male ministers. And she was willing to do whatever it took to get the job done.

While they had sold the weekday show and the VA Beach production facilities, they had brought their best videographers to ESVA with them. These professionals now staffed the new, more modern facility they built here. These professionals traveled with them when needed, to record their live events across the country. These shows had now moved onto the internet instead of being restricted to cable, meaning that they could be produced at their leisure and on their own schedule. Instead of being stuck within the limits of the old show's outline, they had now pivoted and were reaching beyond that with new content, delivered to a worldwide audience.

It was because of Sandra that the take, or as her father preferred to call it, the total of the offerings, had been steadily increasing, and were now even coming from multiple continents. The Mole knew she had been the one with the vision to make this happen, not Marty. His wanting her beside him on stage had been the biggest acknowledgment of that so far. If Marty didn't like it, then tough.

"What did Keller want, father?"

The Mole scowled. "He had the nerve to try and tell me to stop distributing the water, and to shelve the plans for the prayer cube and the event videos."

"Why?"

"He claimed that they would reflect badly on his show and that if we continued, we'd be in violation of our contract terms, and he would sue us for damages."

Sandra thought a minute then said, "First, we're well within our rights since we don't mention the old show in any of it, and because you haven't even been the host of that show for over a year. Sounds more to me like he might've seen the latest ratings; I've heard they aren't good. More likely he's looking for a scapegoat to point to for his investors."

The Mole thought a minute, "You could be right. It sounds like he might be trying to set up something for his defense. He was very self-absorbed when he pulled in here, to the point he almost cut the line on Murphy's tarpon. I saw they had a bit of a scuffle after he left, too."

"Let me handle him from now on, father. I'll see that he doesn't bother you."

The Mole reached over and patted his daughter's arm, just as their cook brought in their plates. Then he took Sandra's hand and said a quick prayer of thanks before they started eating. Again, the prayer was more repetitious than heartfelt, like they had been in the past.

5

THEY'RE BAAAAACK!

Lindsay was slowly, sensuously, kissing my entire face. Then she used her tongue and licked me from chin to forehead. Her breath smelled...bad. "What the hell?" I opened my eyes and saw that Linds had gotten very hairy overnight. It was Tank, of course, wanting to be let out as well as to be given his breakfast, in whatever order each was offered. I got up and "hit the head," then decided it wasn't fair to make him wait while I made my coffee. After putting on shorts and a tee shirt, we both headed out for the grassy area next to C2.

As I opened the houseboat's door, I instantly regretted my choice of clothing. Fall had made a surprise arrival last night; it was now just below sixty degrees outside where the world was covered with dew. My shorts would probably still be the proper attire at around ten o'clock or so, but that was just shy of four hours from now. After a brisk walk with Tank, I'll be back for some jeans and a windbreaker.

Ten minutes later I fed Tank and brewed a "to go" cup of coffee, then he and I headed back out for his second "constitutional" after I changed into jeans. This time it was followed by a more leisurely walk over to the *Cove Restaurant's* patio deck for my breakfast. As we passed the charter dock, it was strange to see so many of the rigs still tied up on a weekend morning. But their crews wouldn't be back from the wedding until later today.

Up on the patio, overhead heaters were fighting to take the damp chill out of the air. As much as I like the more unobstructed view from over by the railing, I chose to park my thin-blooded, native Floridian self in the middle of the deck where it was the warmest. There weren't many other customers here yet, and most of them were sitting inside the warm restaurant, so Tank and I had our pick of tables.

I'd no sooner sat down when I spotted John Rolly from Rolly's Marine in VA Beach walking up the steps. He saw me and came over to my table.

"Hey, John. Having breakfast?" I like John. In his early sixties, a real straight talker, and unapologetically so. He's also one of the best outboard mechanics in the mid-Atlantic. I motioned to the empty chair across from me.

John nodded his acceptance and sat down as he answered, "Yeah, figured I would since I was here. Which'd be thanks to you, from what I hear."

Before I could ask why our server came over and handed out menus then went to grab coffee for the both of us. We quickly studied the menus ordered when she returned. "I'll get that out to you shortly."

After she left, I asked John, "So, how am I the reason you're here?"

"That guy Keller, with *Rev'd Up*. He said, 'that jerk who owns *Mallard Cove*' ran him up onto an oyster bed and made him wipe out a set of wheels."

I could see he was getting a kick out of telling me the story. Oh, and "wheels" is just another word you'll hear used around the docks instead of "propellers."

But now I was mad. "That lying son-of-a-bitch! He rammed me in a narrow channel, bounced off my stern, and ended up on that bar. Then he went for the throttles. What a moron."

"Kinda figured it was somethin' like that, Murph. You should see this guy when he gets in a current or a crosswind at the dock, he goes right for the gas, every time. A real pinball wizard, he bounces off everything. Well, don't worry, I'm charging him triple for a service call to ESVA on a Sunday, so I'm gonna put a hurtin' on his wallet. He damage your boat?"

"I was in Casey's outboard, but no, not even a scratch." I told him the story about how he'd almost cost us our fish.

"Well, that boy's lucky he only got an ice and bait bath. Don't know what I might've done if I'd been in your shoes."

I nodded. "Wonder why he's in such a hurry to get it fixed that he can't wait until tomorrow and pay the regular rate?"

"He said he's got to make a run to Gwynn's Island first thing in the morning to meet up with some partners. Something about an old hotel that's coming up for sale and going by boat would only take a quarter of the time it'd take to drive up there in the morning rush hour. To be honest with ya, I didn't pay that much attention. The guy just likes to hear himself talk, and he doesn't pay me enough to hafta listen to him."

"Yeah, I kind of got that he was full of himself. Has quite a mouth on him too, for a reverend."

John snorted. "Reverend, my ass. Must be one of those mail-order title things. He's a real estate investor. I've got a few other customers that are too, just like you and Casey. Only none of y'all try passin' yourselves off as preachers."

"Wait, a real estate investor?" I said, "I thought he owned that televangelist show."

"Where do you think he got the kind of dough it took to take it off the Mole's hands? The guy buys old hotels and rehabs 'em, supposed to turn 'em into high-end Christian retreats. Then he sells 'em for big bucks, and never pays a dime of tax, 'cause they're part of his 'ministry,' just like the TV show. It's all a racket if you ask me."

"Sounds like it," I agreed. I guess everybody but me must've already known Stoneman's nickname.

"I wonder if I can start a mechanic ministry, then I won't hafta pay taxes neither."

"Somehow John, I don't think that'd pass the IRS 'sniff test.' Though I'd pay big money to watch you give a sermon." We both laughed at the thought.

"I can tell you this much, it'd be one you'd never forget, Murph!"

"No, I don't believe I would."

Our food arrived, cutting off further conversation. Throughout our meal, I was silently reviewing what John had told me. So, Keller bought and sold hotels, eh? That made better sense to me than him being a real minister. John was right, that would be quite a racket. Not only would he not pay tax on any gain, but the second his 'ministry' buys a property, it comes off the real estate tax rolls. Heck, I'd love to keep what we pay in property taxes for *Mallard Cove* every year.

So, Keller was headed to Gwynn's Island over on the west side of the bay in the morning to look at an "old hotel." There was only one property I knew of on that island that fits this description, and it's got an old marina attached. The hotel part has been closed for years, though there are still a few boats in the remaining usable slips of the marina. The story I heard was after the owner died, his surviving family members were all cousins who couldn't get along or agree on what to do with it. After years of paying increasing property taxes with the declining marina income, it sounds like they've finally agreed it needs to go.

I've seen the place once from the water about a year ago, one day when Marlin and I were over there fishing. I got the story about the owners when we stopped for lunch in a waterfront hole in the wall right next door. That old hotel property might fit in well with our investment group's portfolio. One thing Casey and I are good at is fixing up old buildings and marinas. And if Keller was going over there "with some partners," it sounds like he probably scoped it out already and might be showing it to his money people before making an offer. I was going to make sure that the sellers didn't jump at it by setting up an appointment right after theirs to tour the property.

Our group now has five prime properties: *Lynnhaven, Mallard Cove, Cape Charles, the Bluffs,* and *Bayside*. But we don't have anything on the western side of the Chesapeake as of yet. If we can get this at the right price, it could be a home run. But even if we can't, at the very least I want to make sure that Keller has to pay dearly for it. A bit of payback for cutting me off and ramming me.

Okay, you're right, it probably won't teach him anything. But it will sure make me feel a hell of a lot happier. I know, I know, I shouldn't take joy from someone else's misfortune. In this case, I don't care. The more I learn about this guy, the more I despise him. Costing him time and money is going to make my week.

THE TOUR BUS pulled into the lot a little after one o'clock, stopping first up by charter boat row to drop off half its passengers. Then it pulled through the gate that led to the little cove. Tank and I were waiting there, playing "fetch" with a tennis ball in the parking area to kill time. Kari and Marlin were the first two off the bus, and the ball was instantly forgotten. I don't know who was more excited to see who; Tank or his humans. Next off was Sandy Morgan, along with his niece and boat-mate, Micah Monroe. Finally, down came Lindsay, who I wrapped up in a huge, tight hug.

She looked up at me, "Missed you, Babe!"

"Yeah, me too. I've got lots to tell you." I looked over at Kari and Marlin, "You guys, too."

Sandy spoke up, "Is it something worth writing about?"

"To tell you the truth, Sandy, I'm not sure you should."

"Oh, then I'll want to hear it for certain! Let me drop my bags on the boat, and I'll be right over."

Marlin spoke up, "Make it at our place. Tank has a new present, and I know he won't want to go anywhere with it."

"Good. You keep a better brand of beer than Murph anyway."

I looked quizzically at Kari, who then pulled the largest beef-flavored cow bone I'd ever seen from the luggage compartment under the bus. Every inch of Tank was wagging as he latched onto it and headed straight for their houseboat, the *Tied Knot*.

"Yep, that's what I figured would happen." Marlin looked at me, "So, what's the mystery?"

"Tell you in a minute, let me get Lindsay's bag aboard first."

"Meet us up on the party deck. I'll bartend," Kari offered.

"Deal."

FIVE MINUTES later we joined the rest of the group on the open-air third deck of *Tied Knot*. Despite having fed and taken care of him the last few days, Tank ignored me as I passed by, intent on making headway on his dinosaur-sized chew-bone. Sandy and Marlin were already at the bar, working on a pair of Red Stripe beers. Kari was standing behind the bar with a glass of wine in front of her. Seeing us coming, she dug another Red Stripe out of the beer cooler and poured a white wine for Lindsay. We sat in a couple of bar chairs as Kari addressed me with a grin.

"Okay, what trouble did you get into while we were gone?"

"What makes you think I got into trouble," I asked.

"Because I know you, and I know what happens when we aren't here to keep you out of it. Spill the beans, you know that we're going to find out anyhow."

I frowned. "First, let me say that I'm insulted that you think I can't stay out of trouble for only a handful of days without some so-called adult supervision. When, in fact, I sold the biggest listing that the brokerage had while you guys were all off playing."

"Nice, Babe! Congratulations." As a partner in the brokerage, Lindsay knew this was quite a shot in the arm for our latest business, and right before the slow winter season.

Kari nodded, but said, "Yeah, you said 'first'. That's usually the good news, followed by a 'second' with not-so-good news, and if things keep going downhill maybe even a 'third'."

Kari's hazel eyes even seemed to be laughing as she ribbed me. Only in her latter twenties, she was the youngest of our group. Sharp looking too, at five feet six with long black hair down to her mid-back, and very shapely. An ESVA native, she has out-fished everyone here at one time or another, but her biggest attribute is that she's smart. In fact, she's smarter than all of us. Casey and Dawn recognized that right after she went to work for them as a receptionist. This was two years ago, and since then she's been put in charge of designing, building, and managing all their new projects, and is a partner in each of them as well. She was the one who came up with the concept and laid out the site plan for *Mallard Cove*, and she's currently working on two huge projects at Lynnhaven and Cape Charles.

I jokingly frowned at her before telling the story, stopping at the point where I had dinner with Mimi. I saw that Sandy had been taking notes as I spoke.

Kari said, "Yep, this one's going to have a 'third' attached to it."

"Well, you're right. But instead of going downhill, it'll lob a slow pitch right across home plate in front of you." I told them about what I learned at breakfast this morning.

You can almost see the gears turning in Kari's head when she starts to get a project in mind. She is the absolute best at figuring out what's called in real estate the "highest and best use" for a property. After I finished, she waited for a beat before talking.

"Great catch, Murph. I know that property, my family and I spent the night there once when I was a kid. I haven't been over there in a while, but I remember the general layout. Yes, that could end up being a real gem. I'll make some calls tomorrow to find out who the realtor is and get us an appointment to go look it over."

"So, how do I get to become a reverend," Sandy asked. I wasn't sure if he was joking or not.

"That's not the tricky part," I said. "That would be trying to convince the IRS that the *Beach Bar* is a church since their brunch is where you spend most of your Sunday mornings, slurping mimosas."

"Smartass. I never 'slurp'. And it's not like I haven't seen you do the same."

"Just remember when they 'pass the plate' afterward, that's a bill, Sandy, and not putting something in that plate isn't an option." I love needling him.

"Yeah, right. Seriously, there's a good angle here for a book. Developers masquerading as churches? Talk about your tax scammers! I hate people that try to get for free what the rest of us have to pay for, especially when they try to pass themselves off as people who are doing good works. Hey Kari, grab me another Red Stripe, would you? Thanks."

I said, "Yeah, they're almost as bad as beer mooches."

"Who's mooching beers? Oh, right, Sandy's already here." Baloney had just emerged from the stairwell at the end of the deck.

"You're a fine one to talk, Gilligan! You drank a whole brewery's worth of Casey and Dawn's beer this weekend," Sandy accused him.

"And I told you never to call me that again! That was just so you wouldn't drink so much. Which brings up the point..."

"Here you go, Bill." Kari slid a bottle across the bar top as Baloney took his usual unlit cigar out of his mouth and put it in his pocket.

"Thanks, Kari." He turned to me, "I'm not home two minutes and I hear around the docks you put somebody up on the jetty?"

Scuttlebutt moves around a marina faster than a big boat wake. "No, I was the one who got rammed." I gave him a quick summary of my run-in with Keller.

"Then that jerk deserved it. Hey, you think there's any more tarpon up there?" Baloney loves nothing better than having the newest fishing info.

I shook my head, "Doubtful after the cold snap last night. I was surprised to find that one yesterday, and it's probably down past Hatteras by now. But they'll be back in eight months or so."

"Darn. Oh, well, you and I can go after 'em next summer."

"Plan on it. You bring the beer."

"Sounds goo... huh? Oh, right, hah!"

So, I guess I'm going to be on the hook for the gas, the bait, *and* the beer. As usual. Well, I'll worry about that next summer.

Looking around now at my friends, I'm glad that Lindsay and I are no longer on the fishing tournament circuit, and that we're here now year 'round. I'd miss this bunch too much this winter. And when you think back on it, we were very lucky, making enough to get started together in real estate. That more than a thousand-mile cruise to the tip of Florida and back every year takes its toll. I don't know how Sandy does it. Linds and I can find enough adventure right here, in our backyard. Maybe Gwynn's Island will become another one. I know I'm looking forward to finding out.

6

———

GWYNN'S ISLAND

E*arly Monday morning...*

REVEREND DONNY BROOKS was riding with Keller aboard the *Rev'd Up* as they crossed the Chesapeake Bay, headed for Gwynn's Island. He had to raise his voice just slightly to be heard above the wind and the three outboard motors that were mounted a dozen feet behind them.

"Joe, the thing is, Branson has been doing a little digging. He heard the numbers on the show for the next quarter won't be good. Again. This will make the fourth consecutive quarter that the numbers have gone down instead of up. In fact, despite your continued assurances, they haven't gone up since we bought it, and he's not happy."

Branson was the most influential member of their group of "ministry investors," and Brooks often deferred to him. Probably at least in part because he put in the majority of their group's funds and saw himself as the leader. But also, because he was a big, imposing man, and a bully. Though Keller was more worried about the investment side of that equation than the physical one, especially if they could make a deal on this property. They would need his ministry's money since Branson was loaded.

"These things happen, and I'm not happy about it either. There was no way to foresee that new show coming out of Texas on the other network. That guy has a mega-church, so he had a huge audience to start with, and they can now tell their friends across the country to watch on cable and worship right along with them."

Brooks scowled, "And that took a chunk of our audience right off the bat. The drain is continuing. I need to warn you upfront that Branson was furious when he found out. Not the least of it was because he had to dig it up; you didn't tell us. He feels like you're holding out on the rest of us because you either had to know or at least should have known this was going to happen."

"If I had known it would, do you think I'd have put my own ministries' money in it?" Keller was angry about being forced on defense.

"Joe, it was your job to know. You are the television 'expert,' and that's why our ministries invested so heavily with yours. Now it's starting to look like we were all hoodwinked by Stoneman. Like he knew things would be going south after he got out. And another thing, Branson goes nuts every time he sees the ads for that water of his, especially when it's during our show."

"Hey! I can't tell the network what ads they can or can't accept."

"You better find a way to, Joe. I just found out about Stoneman's new 'prayer cube' thing. It's another way to get his face in front of our viewers, selling his own pre-recorded Scripture passages in a little digital player. I don't even want to think about how Branson is going to react to that when he hears about it."

"That's out of my control. He can get as upset as he wants, but it's not going to do him any good. I went up to Stoneman's to try to talk about it, and he just laughed at me. He has container loads of those things on the way from overseas, and he's going to saturate the cable channels with ads for them when they arrive."

Brooks leaned back in his seat, digesting Keller's comments.

Normally he enjoyed boat rides, but not today. There was a nagging sense of dread hanging over this one.

~

Lindsay and I walked into Kari's office. The two large screens on the wall showed different aerial and satellite views of the thirty-acre, triangle-shaped spit of land at Gwynn's Island that held the old hotel and marina.

"Wow, there's a lot more land there than it looked like from the water." I was pleasantly surprised.

Kari nodded. "I didn't remember it being that big either. Then again, I was just a kid when I stayed there."

"What, last year?" I'm in a good mood, and the reactions I get from teasing her can make it even better. The scowl I got in return this morning was exactly what I was hoping for.

Kari shot back, "Are you forgetting that Lindsay is only a couple of years older than me?"

Lindsay patted me on the shoulder and said, "Business, Babe, focus on business."

"Sorry. Guess I'm just happy to have all of you back. Anyway, did you find out who's handling the sale," I asked.

Kari looked insulted, then handed me a copy of the listing, and the price printed at the bottom appeared reasonable. "We have a one o'clock appointment over there."

"One o'clock? What's it, a hundred miles? A two-and-a-half-hour drive," I asked, knowing she already had the answers. Like I said before, she's smart.

"That would be if things aren't backed up around Hampton and the tunnels. But it's only thirty miles up and across the bay. We can make it in an hour in your Merritt. Plus, there's a restaurant on the south side of the bridge that I've heard is great. But we'll need to leave in an hour if you want to have enough time to eat, too."

Her phone rang, and I could see she wasn't happy when she read the caller ID. She picked it up on speaker. "You're supposed to be on your honeymoon, Casey. By the way, you're on speaker with Murph and Lindsay."

"We're underway, heading up the bay for the Chesapeake and Delaware canal. Running gets boring, especially when I'm not at the helm." Casey and Dawn had a full-time professional crew for *Lady Dawn*. "You know me, I'm not much for relaxing on a workday."

I spoke up, "With you, every day is a workday. Congratulations, by the way. Now go back to your honeymoon and let us get to work."

"Thanks, but with you three there together, you're up to something. What're you guys working on?"

Kari said, "Something that may or may not turn out to be an opportunity. Murph is right, you need to get back to your trip. If this pans out, we can talk about it then."

Casey had switched to speaker also. "Dawn's right here with me."

"Hi, guys. Or we can talk about it now. What are you working on?"

The three of us looked at each other, knowing that the two workaholics would keep calling and bugging us until we give in and tell them the details, honeymoon or no honeymoon. I started with the Mole story and handed it off to Kari who finished up with our appointment. There was a long silence, and I could picture the two of them looking at each other, silently questioning the logic of adding this property. Finally, Casey spoke up.

"It's kind of off the beaten path, isn't it? Not a lot of traffic on that island. Maybe it would be better suited for their Christian retreat." He sounded doubtful. "I know that side of the bay is gradually appreciating, but how could we make it pay for itself as we wait for it to do that?"

Kari gave a two-word answer, "*Herring Cove.*"

I knew she already had a plan, though she hadn't even shared it with Linds and me yet. Suddenly it made sense. *Herring Cove* was a competitor up in Maryland that had started with a run-down non-operational hotel and marina. It was also off the beaten path, yet close enough to Washington, DC, about twenty miles south of Annapolis. The group that bought it had recognized the value of a waterfront wedding setting so close to the Capitol and created three separate venues on that campus. They were booked solid from spring until fall every year. Our number one nemesis in the marina and real estate business, Glenn Cetta, had recently purchased the property after we beat him out for the Cape Charles project. Taking him on, at least partly, would appeal to Casey and Dawn. I know it did to everyone else in this room.

There were a few seconds of silence before Dawn said, "Can you bounce us everything?"

"Will do. Give me a minute," Kari replied.

Casey said, "We'll call you back after we look it over." He hung up.

Ever wonder why yachts and sportfishing boats have had an increasing number of satellite domes on their radar arches, hardtops, and tuna towers over the past few years? That's because their owners want to be able to stay in touch, no matter where they are if they're actively involved in their businesses. And being the entrepreneurs that they are, Casey and Dawn have the equivalent of a full office aboard *Lady Dawn*.

Back when I chartered my boat, I had a few CEOs and one Chairman of the Board of some large companies as clients. You could tell who was what by their phone usage. The Chairman's phone seldom rang, and when it did, it was usually a family member or friend. Things at the office were handled by his staff, and he made only the larger decisions, and then usually at board meetings. The CEOs, however, were constantly on the phone or answering emails, and texts. They lived their businesses, twenty-four/seven. These people have to keep in touch if they want to keep their jobs, even when they're out of the office and having fun.

In each of our businesses, we have people who are responsible for various aspects of them. But like the CEOs, every one of us here still "lives" them as well and has that need to keep in touch. None of us truly expected either of those two to shut off their phones while they were on their trip, honeymoon or not. As I said, *Lady Dawn* has her share of satellite domes as well. We waited while Kari loaded an email with files, then sent it.

"Compete with Cetta's *Herring Cove*? I like it already." Lindsay especially despised Cetta, who had tried to hijack our very first deal together for *Mallard Cove*. That had earned him a black and blue bruise on his butt, courtesy of a well-placed throw by Linds with a heavy lead fishing weight. Since that day we have created a lot of history with that man, all of it bad, and the subject of several stories for another day.

"At least we'll draw from around Virginia and especially Richmond."

Kari put a sketch up on the wall screen, showing the proposed sites for three venues on the property. Each could simultaneously hold weddings without any of the guests even being aware of the others. She must've gotten to work early. If we get the property, Cetta will blow a gasket when he hears how we're going to poach at least some of his would-be customers. I can't wait to see how this plays out.

TWO HOURS later I was easing the throttles back on the big V-10 Man diesels in *Irish Luck*, my sixty-foot 1987 Merritt sportfish. We had crossed the bay as a west wind had started to kick up. By the time we ducked into the protected waters between Gwynn's Island and the small town of Hudgins on the mainland, we had begun quartering some six-foot swells that were closely spaced. Not that we felt it too much in the Merritt, other than taking a bit of spray on the flybridge. But the Chesapeake has a well-earned reputation for getting nasty quickly in the fall and winter.

We picked up a "stowaway" back at *Mallard Cove*. Sandy wasn't about to let us leave without being part of "his new story." He wanted to ride along and have lunch at that hole-in-the-wall restaurant named "Bay Breeze" right next to the bridge. I was happy to have the extra hands aboard, since we'll have to give *Irish Luck* a full washdown after we get back, and it'll go faster with all four of us. Nobody rides for free.

We tied up at the end of the restaurant's dock and were early enough to get a table inside overlooking the dock and the water. The new owners of the place had raised the building about six feet and put it on pilings after the property had flooded during a hurricane. Yes, unfortunately, we get those darn storms here too, though not often, and a direct hit is very rare. But they push water out in front of them, and in the bay, it acts like the plunger in a syringe. The farther up the bay you go, the higher the water can get.

The result of raising their building was twofold: dry feet, and a greatly improved waterfront view from the dining room and outside deck. And I have to admit, I love looking out at my boat while I have lunch. Merritts have a classic sportfish look, and they've changed it very little since the Merritt family framed their first hull back in 1955. There was something very pleasing about their lines, and I'm proud of mine.

I caught some movement out beyond my boat and saw a familiar center console emerging from under the span of the swing bridge that was next to the restaurant. *Rev'd Up.* As I watched, it turned toward the restaurant. When they tied up, I saw there were five people aboard: Keller, and four other men. Two minutes later they all walked into the restaurant.

Keller spotted me from the doorway and rushed over to our table. He blurted out angrily, "What are *you* doing here?"

I smiled. "Haven't you heard? The fishing here is great. The bait schools practically jump into your boat. Oh, and we're looking at buying that hotel and marina next door."

I don't know which statement made him angrier, the part about the bait in the boat, or that we might be competing with his group for the hotel property. Then again, it was probably a tie.

"Well, then you've wasted a trip. My reverend friends and I are already going to contract on that property."

I could see this was news to the men standing behind him, and three of them didn't look exactly happy about it. The fourth was smiling broadly, so I'm guessing he's the broker.

The largest man said to Keller, "We need to talk about that, Keller." He led the others to a table across the room, about as far away from us as they could get. Before the smiling man could sit down with them, he was expelled from the group. He looked confused and started for the door, but I waved him over.

"Are you the broker?"

He stuck out his hand, "Yes, Larry Donnelly."

I introduced myself and our group and motioned to the last empty chair at our table. Out of the corner of my eye, I saw Keller staring daggers at me while he and his friends were having a quiet, yet heated discussion. Apparently, the bigger guy hadn't liked Keller running his mouth. He slammed an open hand on the table, stopping conversations at other tables as people turned and stared. This guy was supposed to pass as a preacher? Give me a break.

Kari said, "Reverends, huh? So, Larry, I'm guessing that you don't have an offer from them. How about any others?"

"Uh, well, we've had a lot of interest in the property."

She nodded, "Which has been on the market for over a month so far. But still no offers."

"Well, they are a very interested group." Larry didn't sound all that convinced now.

"Maybe you meant they're an interesting group. Or, if they're that interested in the property, we might be just wasting our time looking at it. I guess we should head back after lunch," I said, though I was just pulling his chain to see how he reacted.

"*NO!* Er, I mean, you're already here. I'll be glad to show you around the property, and you can take all the time that you need."

The poor guy's day had started out so promising, and now he was watching his hopes for any offer from either group evaporating. And it's not surprising that he hadn't had any offers yet on the property, being so far removed from everything. Other than fishing and eating at this restaurant, there wasn't a lot to do here.

The island is only about four miles long by three-quarters of a mile at its widest point, and it has less than a thousand year-round inhabitants. One point of the hotel's triangle-shaped property is closer to the mainland than anywhere else on the island, roughly a thousand feet away. The other side of the island borders the Chesapeake. But it has some great sunsets over that waterfront backdrop, and that's part of what we liked about it. And after wedding season is over, it's right in the middle of some of the best rockfish (striped bass) fishing on the bay.

With it being so isolated, the highest and best uses for the property as a hotel & marina combination would be either as a retreat or as a destination wedding setting. Larry was well aware of this and also knew that his best hope of landing a contract anytime soon rested with one of our two groups. With every day that passed, the clock was ticking down toward the expiration of his listing contract.

"I hear their spicy coleslaw here is good," I said as I saw Larry visibly relax. I wanted to let him off the hook a bit, but not all the way.

"Best on the bay, though I'm not taking anything away from your restaurants."

I nodded, then went back to checking out the menu. Larry must have done his homework, and that makes things easier for us. No need to convince him that any offer from us is for real.

"You can come back to our table now." Keller had come over to retrieve the broker. Larry gave us an apologetic look and got up to follow Keller back. I could see he'd have liked to tell the "reverends" to go to hell, but he was sworn to ethically represent his sellers. Meaning he had to deal with anyone that was a qualified buyer, no matter how obnoxious they were.

I said, more for Keller's benefit than Larry's, "We'll see you around one or so. Though you can catch a ride back around the bridge on our boat if you want." I motioned toward my Merritt. Keller glanced back, irritated. Then he looked past me and out the window, and for a second his irritation seemed to turn to envy. Then he marched back over to his table, now with Larry in tow.

FOLLOWING A GREAT LUNCH, after leaving the dock I called for a bridge opening on the VHF radio. While we waited for the gates to drop and the span to swing open, Keller and his boatload passed us. With no tower or flybridge, they cleared the still-closed span with a foot or two to spare. By the time we pulled up to the hotel's docks just beyond the bridge, he had dropped off all but one of his passengers, including Larry. He passed us again, headed in the opposite direction but staring straight ahead like we didn't exist. Glad that I didn't have to listen to one of *that* guy's sermons. Not that I truly believe he's ever preached in any church in his life.

Larry caught our stern lines as we tied up.

"Beautiful boat, Mr. Murphy."

"Just Murph, Larry. And thanks."

"Murph it is then. Well, I've got the keys to everything with me. As I said, you all can take your time looking the place over. Where would you like to start?"

WE SPENT the next two hours looking over the buildings, both inside and out. It was going to take a full rehab, from roofs to drywall and insulation, but I'd done over a dozen projects like this with Casey back in Florida, not to mention what we've done since we arrived in Virginia a couple of years ago. So, Kari took a lot of pictures and videos, since we knew that Casey and Dawn would want to give it a thorough look.

We cast off after saying goodbye to Larry and telling him we'd contact him in the morning after we had time to talk over the property. This time we didn't go back through the bridge but turned to the right, heading out to the mouth of the Piankatank River, which borders the north side of the island. Then it was back out into the bay, though this time we'd have a much drier ride, going downwind and down-sea.

Sandy came up the flybridge ladder with one of my Red Stripes in hand. I figured he would since I had stocked the 'fridge before we left. He settled in next to Lindsay on the flybridge's "U" shaped wrap-around couch in front of the helm.

Lindsay cocked her head slightly as she looked at me and Kari, who was in the helm chair to my left. "What did you guys think?"

Kari replied, "It has possibilities. But it would take a lot of work, so we have to get it at the right price. I'm a little worried that Keller and company might be willing to pay more than us since they won't have the tax issues we will."

I nodded in agreement. "Both real estate as well as corporate. The benefits of them being a church."

Sandy snorted. "Church, my ass. Saw 'em say grace before they ate, but it wasn't for real. I'd bet that's about as close as they get to preaching. If you ask me, they're just a bunch of damn tax-dodging developers. No offense about the developer part."

I said, "None taken. I think you're right. That big ape who was pounding the table sure wasn't acting like any preacher I've ever met."

"More like a loan shark's leg breaker," Linds remarked.

I said, "Pretty much. It's funny, at least the Mole carries on like a preacher, even though he's at best a corrupt one. He had bonafide roots in religion at one time, way back when. But the more I see of Keller and his crew, the less I believe that's how they must've started.

"I've met my share of scumbags in the real estate business who probably wouldn't hesitate to try and pull this scam, except for being unsure about carrying it off. Then there's that famous case about the preacher whose spectacular downfall as a developer helped lead to some serious jail time, and that was no doubt quite a deterrent. But Keller's guys were well-versed in the ins and outs, and they knew just how far they could push the tax envelope. Probably with plenty of good advice from bad lawyers. Here's hoping that they end up making a misstep and get snagged."

Sandy raised his beer, "Amen, brother Murph, amen."

7

———

TAKE IT OR...

"So, what do you two think?" Kari asked. She, Linds, and I had reconvened in her office after we got *Irish Luck* all washed and squared away, having lost Sandy to the *Cove Beach Bar*. Kari now had Casey and Dawn on a video call after she forwarded the pictures and videos to them.

"It has possibilities, but it looks like a lot of work. The purchase price will make it or break it," Dawn said.

"That's what we all agreed," Kari told them the price the three of us had decided on.

"That's where I'd start, too," Casey said.

Kari shook her head. "Not with that other group circling around. This is a 'drop dead' offer, with a forty-eight-hour window for acceptance, and loaded with plenty of contract 'outs' for us during the due diligence period. I'm not interested in getting into a bidding war. We tie it up fast or forget it."

"We'll leave it to you guys; you sound like you are on the right track. Let us know what happens," Casey seemed pleased with the way Kari was thinking.

"I want us all to sleep on it before we make an offer," Kari said.

Casey nodded. "That's never a bad idea, especially with a 'drop

59

dead' offer. Helps them understand you're serious when you don't appear to be in a hurry. Call or text us when you hear something." With that, the video link ended.

A LITTLE LATER OVER AT the *Beach Bar*, Linds and I saw Rev sitting with Sandy, and we took the two empty chairs at their table.

"Well? Did you buy it or what?" Sandy wanted an update.

"Not yet, we all want a night to sleep on it," Lindsay replied.

Rev nodded thoughtfully. Sandy must have told him about our trip. "You know, that's something that I've advised a lot of my parishioners to do who have come to me for guidance. There's that old but wise saying about 'act in haste, repent at leisure.' Especially with such a large purchase."

Lindsay added, "And when we're planning on making one offer, not entering into a long negotiation process."

He nodded at her, "Exactly."

I spoke up, "You should have seen the guys Keller brought with him. His partners are all supposed ministers, but I don't buy that for a second. The one guy was a bruiser, and made Keller look polite."

Rev said, "A lot of ministers study divinity in college and seminary, having started down the path early on. But not everyone. Don't forget that in my case, when I started going to my church, this is what turned my life around. I began studying on my own with no specific goal in mind, just a newfound thirst for spiritual knowledge. Our last minister took note of this and started helping direct my studies. But I was still caught off-guard when I was asked to take his place when he retired. I figured I was a bit too rough around the edges to ever become a minister. But our church leaders knew this was exactly what would allow me to relate to our parishioners, as someone who has 'been there and done that.' And they figured my approach might be able to get a few others to join the flock.

"Anyway, that's when I found out that some Christian denominations like mine can hold their own ordination ceremonies, which is exactly what happened to me. And there are online services for nondenominational ordination as well, some requiring studies, and others that don't. So, I'm not going to be quick to judge the validity of someone else's ordination, that's out of my wheelhouse."

"Yeah, like the Mole's," I said.

"That one I do know a bit about. Like I told you before, he got chatty when he tried buying our church. He's from a long line of evangelicals. He grew up preaching with his parents, traveling across the country for years, and doing tent revivals. Then he discovered the prosperity gospel and broke away from his parent's ministry to form his own which was based on it."

"What the heck is the prosperity gospel," I asked. "You mentioned that the other day."

"It's one interpretation of the gospel that says that any money you donate to a church or ministry will come back to you in a multiple of that amount, and that's the big reason for giving. But I can tell you that it's not my interpretation. Yes, I believe it's good and right to give to the church, but not just so you can make money back from it.

"I believe what you are supposed to get from it is purely spiritual, not monetary. It should make you feel good. And the money you give should be used to maintain the church, perpetuate its spiritual teaching, and also help those in need within the community, starting within our congregation. But you can see in the Mole's ads that while some of the people testify to having kicked drugs or alcohol, the big focus for these folks is on getting new cars, bigger boats, and houses, as well as receiving 'surprise' checks that appear out of thin air." Rev shook his head sadly. "People believe what they see on those ads because they desperately want it to happen to them."

I asked, "So if the Mole and Keller are on the same wavelength, why would they have been fighting on the dock?"

"From what I've heard, Keller and his group had thought the Mole would just fade away quietly and retire after he sold them the show and studio. They had no clue he would start up that mystical water thing, his 'outreach ministry.' Even though he doesn't mention his old show in his ads, people will always associate him with it.

"Keller and his group just found out it's about to go beyond the water thing; he has a ton of 'prayer cubes' pre-recorded with his voice, reciting bible verses and prayers. Plus, he and his kids are putting together a big schedule of personal appearances. These are part revival, and part new product promotion with videos of these events for sale online. Plus, he has a book about to come out."

"So, they're torqued off," I said.

"Ohhh, yeah."

"How do you know all this?"

Rev said, "One of my newer parishioners used to work for the Mole's organization. Her conscience finally began to outweigh what he was paying her, which wasn't all that much anyhow. And don't look at me like that. I'm not betraying a confidence; she shared this with the whole congregation. She wanted to make sure that none of them were ever tempted by any of his ads."

Sandy had been silent through all this. He had his small notebook out that he carried with him everywhere and was busy taking notes.

I asked, "More for your book?"

"Magic water and prayer cubes. Are you kidding me? You can't make this stuff up! Most of what I get around the docks is about fishing, boats, or both. If I'm lucky somebody gets caught onboard 'in flagrante delicto' by a jealous spouse or lover and makes a scene. But this stuff is golden!"

"Are you a reporter, or a writer now," Lindsay joked, half seriously.

"Lindsay, did you ever hear that phrase, 'The truth is stranger than fiction?' The best fiction is based on wild-assed things that come straight from reality. And right now, I can't think of anything stranger than this!"

KELLER WAS BACK in his office at the production studio with Brooks. On the ride back across the bay, they had agreed on a purchase price they knew would secure the Gwynn's Island property. The asking price. It was ten percent higher than they would have liked to settle for if they were the only interested party. But it ensured that they could go to contract unless that Murphy guy wanted to start a bidding war. It irritated Keller that this guy was becoming such a pain and that he might end up costing him a bundle. It seemed like a strange coincidence that he would show up, looking at that property at the same time they were. He wondered how he had found out about it.

"Joe, let's call Branson and Canton and get this over with. I know he's not going to be happy with the price." Donny Brooks was concerned, he saw the potential in the property, but Branson was well known for always wanting a deal, and not being afraid of being forceful to get it. Even resorting to using violence if necessary.

Keller snorted, "Even if it were free that moron would still gripe about it. After we get it all renovated this winter and booked up for next season, he won't be happy then, either. Between you and me, I'm getting tired of him."

Brooks chided him, "But not tired of him putting in three-quarters of the cash into our projects."

"He just got lucky being in Myrtle Beach before property values exploded as they did. Picking up as much acreage as he did back then, it'd be next to impossible not to come out smelling like a rose. Then creating that Christian resort and theme park was a no-brainer. It's not like he's smart. You and I are the ones who have been bringing him the good deals and ideas," Keller said.

"Yeah, and without him putting us onto the whole ministry and church angle, we'd still be paying taxes on our projects and profits. And together we'd still only have that one property in Myrtle Beach. So, yeah, he *is* that smart, and we *do* owe him."

Keller scowled at his fellow "reverend," still not willing to concede the point. Like him, Donny Brooks had become ordained through a website on the internet. No studying was necessary, and it provided a nice paper trail to back up his claim in case of an audit. Since then, both of them had made sure to pray before every meal out in public and to open each meeting with others with a prayer as well. More justification for their tax-exempt status. The truth was that neither was a person of true faith, just convenience.

Both had moved up to Virginia from South Carolina when the group purchased the TV show. They saw the area around the bay as being undervalued and were anxious to grab as much of it as they could before the prices inevitably go up. And no one had tried the Christian resort angle before in the area. They hoped to use it on several properties before anyone else caught on.

Keller dialed Branson's number, knowing that he and Ronald Canton would still be driving back together on I-95 for several more hours. He picked up on the second ring.

"Yeah?"

"Tom, Donny, and I have been hashing this out together, and we think the smart play is to go ahead and give them a full-price offer."

"Oh, you do, do you? Full price. And why don't we all get 'sucker' tattooed on each of our foreheads while we're at it."

"You know it's worth it, and if we don't, we risk getting into a bidding war with Murphy and his group."

"Just who is this Murphy guy, anyhow?" Branson's mood had gone sour.

"I dug into him. His group has five big waterfront properties, including *Bayside Resort and Spa*. One of the partners is Eric Clarke, that billionaire from northern Virginia. Wouldn't you like to be known as the guy who beat him out of this property?" Keller was appealing to Branson's biggest soft spot, his ego.

"Yeah, by paying the full sucker price for it." Branson's voice at first dripped with sarcasm, but then in a more level tone he asked, "Are you sure about Clarke being in on this?"

Keller glanced at Brooks and smiled. He knew he'd just landed Branson. "Absolutely. He's in on all their projects and has a big house over at *Bayside*. If we strike first with a full-price offer, we could get this under contract before they can even react."

"Do it." The phone went dead.

❧

THE NEXT MORNING after a quick call to all the other partners, Kari called Larry with their offer, which was ten percent below asking.

"I'm sorry, Kari, but I received another offer last night that's significantly higher. If you want to raise yours this morning, I think I can get the sellers to hold off long enough for you to talk with your other partners."

Kari shot back, "I don't need to talk with my partners, I can tell you that it's not worth more than that to us."

"Well, I'm sorry, I wish you had ended up with it. I know your reputation for high-level property renovations, and I'd love to have seen you do that with the old hotel. Hopefully, this other group will do the same."

"Hopefully. Well, thanks for your time."

Lindsay and I had heard the conversation on speaker. While I was disappointed, I knew we had to stick to our price.

"Either those guys are going to do a half-assed job on that property, or their tax situation is that much of an advantage," I said.

"Or both," Lindsay said.

"Well, we did what we could. We were dead on with our numbers to be able to do the full renovation and still make money. So, next!" Despite not getting the property, Kari remained upbeat. It's part of what I loved about working with her.

I looked at my watch, Lindsay and I had a meeting in fifteen minutes with a great candidate for a yacht brokerage management position. She's one of the best in the mid-Atlantic. If we hire her, I'm not going to have to be spending as much time at the brokerage anymore. Fingers crossed. And later this morning the Mole's new Westport is getting hauled out for a survey up at Albury's, and I need to make an appearance. Having a busy morning was helping take some of the sting out of losing that property.

"THAT WAS a fine fish you caught behind my home, Murph, surely one of God's most fabulous creations."

The morning had started looking up when we hired our new broker. But when I arrived at Carlton Albury's boatyard, I found the Mole walking around the hull of the Westport, which had just been hauled. So much for improving my mood.

"Yessir, indeed they are. And your home is about as far north as you'll find them. I was hopeful but surprised when we found that last one this late in the year. I'm sure they're all long gone now after our cold snap."

Stoneman looked disappointed, "Oh. I was hoping to talk you into going with me on my outboard to fish for them."

I'd rather fish with a boatload of skunks. Rabid ones. "Unfortunately, they won't be back for another eight months or so."

"Well, I'm not going anywhere, and my new yacht is going to stay at your marina, so we'll be seeing a lot of each other before then."

Oh, goody. At least I have eight months between now and then to make up an excuse not to go. "Thanks in advance for your business. Have you made any plans for cruising this fall? Maybe taking the boat south?"

"Not this year. I have a lot going on in the next few months and being able to come down to *Mallard Cove* and decompress is going to be a nice change. That's part of why I named her *Privacy*. She's going to be my place to escape; to be able to be around the waterfront without actually being seen in public and having to put up with all of what that entails."

I nodded. Maybe this won't be that bad after all. If we don't see him when he's around and he stays aboard his boat, I'll be a happy man.

8

ONE IN EVERY MARINA

F*riday, three weeks later...*

"HE WANTS us to meet him on his *yacht* this afternoon? I guess we paid for that thing, too!"

Branson was disgusted, he and Canton were back in Virginia Beach to go over the show's numbers with their two partners. Last quarter had turned out to be far worse than expected, and the forecast for the current one was dismal. If this kept up, by mid-next year they would be forced to make some big cash infusions just to keep it on the air. Right after receiving this news, he saw another of the Mole's mystical water ads. He went ballistic, demanding that Keller set up a meeting with Stoneman, which he'd reluctantly done.

During the call Keller learned about the new yacht, and that it was docked at *Mallard Cove*, which is where the Mole was willing to meet. As if the show's numbers and the mystical water weren't both upsetting enough. Keller hoped things wouldn't be further compounded by running into that Murphy character over there. He could see that the meeting location rubbed Branson the wrong way.

"I can't help what the man spent the money on. If he wants to be that conspicuous, that's his problem," Keller said.

Branson bristled, "Unless we're the chumps that financed it along with that water setup of his, then it's our problem. You'd better hope and pray we can talk him out of it, or else!"

That statement made Keller both angry and afraid. He'd seen Branson's temper in action before, but fortunately, it had always been directed at someone else. He hoped it would be this time as well.

THE MOLE CAUGHT me off guard when he called and asked if I had plans for lunch, which is why I ended up eating with his kids and him aboard *Privacy*. This was the first time I'd met his son and daughter, who looked to be in their middle thirties. Martin Junior was nothing to write home about, but the daughter was both pretty and smart. It was her that made lunch bearable as she seemed to not have a part in any agenda and was pleasant to talk to.

However, I ended up fielding a bunch of questions from her father about *Bayside*. The three were leaving for there in the morning, taking an inaugural cruise in the new yacht. He had signed them all up for some spa time and high-dollar pampering at the resort. He hinted around that he'd like some special treatment when he arrived, but I wasn't biting. I told him that I was no longer involved with that particular property and didn't have any "pull" there. No sense in telling him that the management companies of both *Mallard Cove* and *Bayside* were interrelated.

I was sure this favor ask was why I had been invited to lunch, but I soon found out it was a "twofer" when one of the crew led Keller and friends back to the salon. The look on Keller's face probably matched mine, which must've looked like I had just bitten into a lemon. In contrast, the Mole looked quite pleased with himself. I quickly thanked them for lunch and got the hell out of there. On my walk down the dock, I realized the Mole had planned to use me to unnerve Keller since they were meeting for business. A sharp move when you think about it, and if you don't mind using people. Not exactly what you would expect from a preacher, but I already knew this guy was no longer a minister, but he had become a huckster.

"Before we get started, Martin, I need to use the head."

"Of course. You can use the crew's head, forward of the galley and down the stairs." Stoneman smiled, knowing that Keller would be passing the more elaborate guest head without being aware of it while on his way down to the crew's.

If Keller picked up on the slight, he didn't show it. But he took his time before returning, knowing that there was no way that Branson could hold his temper in check for this long. He was right, and he could already hear him shouting on the return trip back through the galley. Stoneman's voice was elevated, but Branson was yelling.

"You are violating the intent of our purchase contract!"

Stoneman shot back, "I haven't violated anything. Our contract has a five-year no-compete clause, meaning that I cannot own or appear on any similar cable show as long as your group owns it, and I have honored that." He took a sip of his ever-present cup of chamomile tea with elvish honey. The combination was supposed to help lower his sky-high blood pressure. Though at over twelve hundred dollars an ounce for this world's most expensive honey, there were much more cost-effective remedies available from big pharma. But he delighted in saying to people that he didn't take any medications, and bragged about how each cup of the mixture cost more than filling the gas tank of their car. Keller eyed the tea with disgust, not envy. Stoneman didn't notice.

"Your ads are all over cable and the internet," Branson countered.

"Our contract doesn't say a thing about ads for unassociated products," Sandra stated.

"It's capitalizing on his image, which associates him with our show, and he can't do that!"

Sandra was as cool as they come, and the Mole was enjoying watching her. "Look, Mr. Branson, you paid for a show and a production facility. You got both. You also paid for my father not to go into direct competition with you for five years. Again, you are getting what you paid for, as he hasn't started a new show nor appeared in any existing one. But you did not pay him to sit idle for those five years, and he would never have agreed to that if you had tried."

"I'll sue you for breach of contract, Stoneman!" Branson was trying to reengage the elder Stoneman and make an end-run around his daughter but without success. The Mole was happy to defer to Sandra, who had just slipped an unchallenged or unnoticed "mister" rather than "Reverend" in front of Branson's name.

"It sounds more like something that you need to take up with your lawyer, since he didn't include any of it in the contract. But we haven't breached anything," Sandra said. "We've kept to the letter of the agreement."

"Clint, Mark, would you two please show these gentlemen off my yacht and down the dock, we have a *Bayside* cruise tomorrow to plan for," the Mole said. His two crewmen had been hanging almost invisibly in the background, but now they moved toward Branson. His three companions had remained silent and hadn't displayed a threatening posture as he had, so they weren't a focus. For a second or two it appeared that Branson would try to fight the crewmen until Keller grabbed one of his arms and started pulling him toward the door. Branson violently shook off his hand then stormed out with the other three close behind him.

I WAS glad to get the heck out of there, and more than a little perturbed at being used like that to soften up the Mole's adversary. In the future, I won't be spending any additional time aboard *Privacy*, nor with her owner. If he doesn't like that, as far as I'm concerned, he can keep his yacht up at *Bayside* permanently.

But now I had more important things on my mind and walked over to *C2*. Linds was over there in her "full organizer mode." Casey and Dawn were due back in a few hours, they were on the last leg of their honeymoon trip, coming in from Ocean City. And we were throwing a surprise welcome home party.

I know what you're thinking, we should just let them relax and catch their collective breath after such a long trip. If they had been coming back from a four-week multi-leg airplane trip, we would have. After all, they would need to unload the plane and unpack after they got home. There would be laundry to do, and trip exhaustion to get over. But the Shaws had stayed home, and just watched the scenery change as their home passed it by. Their crew ran the boat, made the meals, cleaned the clothes, and took care of all the details just like they do here every day since Casey and Dawn live-aboard *Lady Dawn* full time. They don't own a house.

As wealthy as they are now, having crossed the line now into the nine-figure territory, they live differently than most people. Heck, they even live differently than other folks with the same net worth. There had been only one time in his life when Casey had lived in a "conventional" way.

Casey Shaw started life as an orphan, raised within the foster care system in Palm Beach County, Florida. He became emancipated at sixteen, got his GED, then went on to take classes at night at the local community college. This was in addition to holding down a job at a boatyard and putting in more hours there than anyone else. Back then his home was an old scow with no motor, and his bed was one side of the vee-berth up in the bow. His slip rent was included as part of his pay from the boatyard.

Casey's work ethic came to the attention of a man named Dave Chauncey, one of the area's biggest real estate investors. He kept his boat at that same boatyard and ended up befriending Casey. Ironically, Dave was also an orphan who started out on his own at an early age. Twenty years Casey's senior, he showed him the real estate ropes. In his first deal, Casey partnered with Dave to option a property in an area that was ripe for redevelopment. When they flipped the option, Casey made the equivalent of three years' pay in less than a week, thanks to Dave's knowledge and direction. He quit his job at the boatyard, went full-time into real estate investment, and never looked back.

A few deals later Casey bought his only house, a beautiful place on the Loxahatchee River in Jupiter, Florida. Other than in the various foster homes, this was the only time he ever lived ashore. Then he married the wrong girl and later lost the house to the girl. He moved back aboard, this time onto an old thirty-one-foot Bertram. Fortunately for him, Dave was right there to help pick up the pieces. He was much more than just a mentor; he had become the father figure Casey never had. They both ended up living in the same marina in Rivera Beach, Florida, aboard their separate boats.

Casey's early life and the episode with his cheating wife added fuel to his introversion and deep-rooted fear of crowds. Back then he could count all of his friends on one hand. The same could be said about long-term girlfriends in those first fifteen years that I knew him. His business had become his spouse, and he lived it seven days a week, except when the fishing was good. Not exactly a recipe for relationship success.

But as the deals got larger so did the boats, for both Casey and Dave. It wasn't about bragging rights for either of them, but all about comfort. Then seventeen years ago, he hired me off the docks to take care of his then-current boat, a fifty-eight-foot Hatteras named *Migration*. He started teaching me about the real estate business, too. We found that we worked great together. But finally, Casey had enough of the crime and congestion that had moved into the area. He cashed out of his Florida properties, purchasing what would become *Bayside* here on ESVA.

Again, he married the wrong woman, an ESVA native named Sally. I tried to warn him about her, but he couldn't see what I saw. Didn't want to see it. I was engaged to Dawn about that time, but I soon met Lindsay, and I knew she was who I really should be with. You might say I handled things badly with Casey, Dawn, and Lindsay at that point, because I did. Meanwhile, things began blowing up for Casey as well. Dave and his wife were murdered; victims of a carjacking in South Florida gone wrong. And when Casey and Sally split, I wasn't around for him like Dave had been before. But fortunately, Dawn was. She not only pulled him out of his funk but also worked with him to get over his fear of crowds. This turned out to be a very necessary thing when they opened *Bayside* and needed to host large promotional events to help get it going.

Dave's death impacted Casey in many different ways. There was a huge personal sense of loss, of course. But since Dave's wife had died seconds before him, Casey became his sole beneficiary. In addition to his ninety-nine-foot Burger yacht and Cessna Citation jet, he left Casey a real estate portfolio worth high eight-figures. Obviously, for most people, this would be enough to make them want to sit back and take it easy for the rest of their lives. Not Casey. For him, the business had never been about being a means to an end, but it was something he did that he enjoyed. Making money wasn't the point; that was just a pleasant side effect. Buying and selling properties was as necessary to him as eating and breathing. And Virginia was a state ripe with deals and opportunities.

But I was off on my own, working hard to make a living around the water. Somehow, I managed to get Lindsay back, only a few months after she broke up with me. We discovered the two of us made a great fishing team, chartering my first boat together and successfully trading up for larger and larger boats. We started fishing high-dollar tournaments ourselves up and down the east coast. When we won the richest billfish tournament in the country, the purse we took home that day let us buy a very run-down *Mallard Cove Marina*.

But the real win in that tournament was when Lindsay and Dawn ended up bonding, in one very rum-soaked celebration aboard *Lady Dawn*. This then paved the way for Casey and me to rekindle our friendship, as well as to go into business together with the *Mallard Cove* property. We're all tighter than ever now. Well, kind of. Dawn still doesn't fully trust me, and I don't know if she ever will. I can't say I blame her. Though I probably know her better than anyone other than Casey and Linds.

Anyway, when *Lady Dawn* ties back up in her slip this afternoon,

I know Casey and Dawn will still be rested and refreshed from their cruise. I also know they'll have missed C2 and hanging out with the gang. And with the usual fall temperatures kicking in, Casey is going to want to have a fire in the fire pit; it's on the list of his favorite things. So is cooking in his outdoor kitchen, which I'm setting up with a pile of ribeye steaks, and a mound of extra-large Virginia shrimp, all ready and waiting for their turn on the wood-fired grill.

Casey has discovered that he likes cooking for his expanding group of friends. This is thanks again in large part to Dawn helping him overcome his fear of crowds. Our "welcome home" gift is to have everyone here and everything ready when they arrive, so he can jump in, cook and entertain. Lindsay was walking out of the "clubhouse" when I got there.

"Hey, Babe, how was lunch with the reverend?" She recoiled a bit when she read my face. "I thought you liked him?"

"Wrong reverend. Mine's a real one. This was the Mole." I filled her in on the details.

"Well, at least they'll be Cindy's problem for the next few days."

I nodded. Cindy Crenshaw was one of our business partners and friends. She ran the hospitality side of all the properties. She'd be arriving later with her partner, Rikki Jenkins, who owns *ESVA Security*, a company that provides security for corporations as well as a lot of very high-profile and uber-wealthy individuals. That's the side of Rik's business which is well known. But the largest part of it is more clandestine; government "projects" that can't be allowed to be connected with the government. In other words, Rikki is one of the largest purveyors of "plausible deniability" inside the DC beltway.

Rik and Cindy live together aboard their fifty-two-foot Hatteras up at *Bayside*, though they have our brokerage quietly looking for something a little larger for them. They're both good at what they do. *Extremely* good. That's why I knew Cindy would handle the Mole and his bunch with no problem, though I'll still give her a "heads up" tonight so she isn't caught flat-footed.

"As much as I like the dockage income, I wish he was permanently Cindy's problem."

"There's always going to be someone like him in every marina, you know that. If we're lucky, it'll stay at only one," Lindsay said.

"He counts as two."

She laughed, "Okay, two. But he's not our problem this afternoon, and we still have work to do. You need to go set up on the jetties."

I grinned since this is something I'm looking forward to. I retrieved a big box from the guest suite and headed for the rocky points on both sides of the little cove's inlet.

9

———

ANOTHER UNION REUNION

"Murph isn't answering his phone," Casey said, disappointed. "I've been trying to reach both Lindsay and Kari, and I keep getting their voicemails, too. I hope everything's all right," Dawn replied.

Both were up on the flybridge deck along with their golden retriever, Bimini, as *Lady Dawn* approached from the south, skirting Fisherman Island. The yacht's captain, Frank Cunningham, aimed the yacht for the mouth of the Virginia Inside Passage, giving the Shaws a great view of *Mallard Cove's* beach as they passed. They could see that both beach bars were starting to build their now somewhat smaller Friday afternoon fall crowds. Frank hugged the eastern shoreline of the cut as they entered, preparing for his tight turn to port into the small cove's inlet several hundred yards ahead.

As they approached, Casey looked beyond the rip-rap breakwater and jetties, scanning the docks and C2, none of which showed any signs of life. Frank then slowly and very carefully executed his turn, making his way into the center of the narrow inlet. His crew prepared the dock lines at various stations on the yacht.

"Murph and Lindsay knew when we were supposed to arrive, and we're right on time. I don't get why we can't even reach them on the phone," Casey said, disappointed. Suddenly, a series of explosions sounded from the rocks on either side of the yacht. "What the hell?"

Light clouds of smoke appeared from the rocks right before numerous firework mortars exploded overhead, causing Bimini to start a fit of barking. More fireworks then launched from the patio deck at *C2*, as people started to stream out of the clubhouse. Frank replied with several long blasts of *Lady Dawn's* huge air horns. A highly decorated golf cart arrived at the covered parking area adjacent to *Lady Dawn's* slip, with Lindsay at the wheel and me sitting beside her.

Bimini quieted down as the noise subsided, and Frank and the crew expertly docked the yacht, then lowered her gangway. Before they went ashore Dawn said to Frank, "I'm glad your concentration wasn't thrown off by those mortars as we came in."

Frank laughed. "The crew and I were expecting them. Murph texted us a heads-up yesterday, but we didn't want to spoil his surprise by saying anything."

Bimini was the first one down the gangway, rushing over to Linds and me.

"Hey, Bim! Did you miss us?" Lindsay patted him on his head as he gazed up at her and then at me with a silent but adoring look.

Dawn rushed over to a hug from Lindsay, as I grasped Casey's hand and gave him a one-armed "bro hug."

"Welcome home, you two, er, three," I said.

Dawn looked over the cart, which was covered in ribbons, flowers, and a "Just Hitched" sign, along with several beer can strings trailing behind it.

"Murph, you are such a child."

"Hey, I didn't do the cart, that was Lindsay. I did the fireworks!"

"I know that. I was talking about the fireworks." She caught me slightly off guard as she hugged me, then backed up half a step, looking into my eyes. "And I'd have been disappointed if you hadn't done something juvenile."

"Of course I did, I'm not dead yet. Hey, load aboard, there's a party going on, and you guys are the guests of honor. And Case, I have an apron waiting on you, since you're 'Chef Casey' on the grill tonight."

The grin Case gave me said that I'd hit it out of the park with the cookout idea. The four of us piled into the cart as Tank came running over to greet Bimini, happy that his canine pal was back. They roughhoused as they ran along behind us, bumping into each other, happy that things were getting back to normal. The twenty-one-acre compound is all fenced with hog wire, allowing the two of them to safely have the run of the place. Casey lightly slapped me on the back, reinforcing how happy he was to be home.

The change in Casey over the past couple of years was no more evident than when we offloaded at C2. Where he once had been able to count his friends on one hand, now he'd have to take off his shoes, and he'd still run out of digits. He and Dawn waded into the crowd, both with big smiles. I stopped and watched while Linds slid her hand in mine, tilting her head slightly as she looked at me.

"Not going to get a drink?" She asked.

"In a minute. Just watching them. If you'd known Casey five years ago, you wouldn't have believed this would be possible."

"You said he was shy."

I shook my head slightly. "No, shy isn't the right word. Dave used to say that Casey was as comfortable alone as he was with somebody. Shy would only mean uncomfortable. Look at him now with Dawn, he's not that guy anymore. I can't imagine him without her."

"Kind of like the way we think about you two," Rikki said. She and Cindy had just arrived and had quietly walked up behind us.

As we exchanged hugs, Lindsay said, "We could say the same about you guys."

"And we can stand here and yak, or we can all go grab drinks and join the party," I added.

Cindy said, "Lead on, McMurph! There's a wine glass over there with my name on it."

As we started toward the patio, we heard a helicopter approaching from back over the woods. A minute later Eric Clarke's red Sikorsky S-76 touched down on the helicopter pad Casey had added next to C2. Eric, his teenage daughter Missy, and his girlfriend, ex-congresswoman Candi Ryan all climbed out and walked over to the party, having flown directly here from Eric's business in Northern Virginia.

If you think that Casey and Dawn's life is well, different, by them being centi-millionaires, you should breathe some of the rarified air that surrounds Eric, who is worth well over twenty-five times that amount. Not that you'd know just in talking with him that he has a dime more than Lindsay and I did when we started a couple of years ago, chartering and living aboard that first old boat. But then you see the big house up at *Bayside*, the helicopter, the Gulfstream jet, vintage Trumpy yacht, and how people who don't even know him treat him like he's special, then you know he's rich. *Really* rich.

However, if you start treating him differently than you would me, it's the quickest way to get kicked out of his orbit. To him, all that stuff is, well, just *stuff*. Tools to help him enjoy life. And he only gets impressed with people and how they act, not things. The three of them made a beeline for Casey and Dawn, then even before they went to the bar, they made a point to come over and say hi to Linds and me.

Now, before you get the wrong idea about Missy, you need to know that she's like most other teens. Kind of. Except that she's exceptionally polite, uses a fraction of the "screen time" that the majority of kids her age do, and fits very well into most conversations with adults or other kids. In one word, she's "impressive."

She's also becoming a great angler in her own right, with Casey, Dawn, Lindsay, and me all teaching her. Not that we're pushing her, she's become obsessed with the sport and is always ready to go with us at the drop of a hat. We put her on her first white marlin two summers ago, and she turned out to be a natural. This last summer she even caught one on a fly rod. An impressive feat for any angler, especially one that isn't even old enough to drive yet.

I wish that I had the natural instinct for fishing that she possesses. We have a surprise in store for her next summer to put those instincts to work, teaming her up with Dawn, Kari, and Lindsay and entering them in a couple of local tournaments as the *Mallard Cove Women's Fishing Team*.

~

FROM THE OPEN aft deck rail, the Mole watched silently as the large white yacht approached from the south. When it turned to enter the Virginia Inside Passage, he saw that it was about the size of his, but he wondered where it might be headed. As it passed, he saw the name on the stern was *Lady Dawn*, and her hailing port was *Bayside, Virginia*.

"She's a beauty, isn't she?" Sandra had joined him at the rail. Like her father, she appreciated boats and the water. Her brother did not and had been against them buying *Privacy* from the start.

"Yes. Yes, she is. I wonder where she's headed, maybe Albury's boatyard," the Mole replied. He wasn't aware of any marinas in Magothy Bay that could handle a boat of her size.

They watched as her course changed just before she went out of sight, seemingly headed for the shore. A few seconds later they heard explosions, and even in the daylight, they could see the flashes of fireworks appearing above the woods at the far end of the marina. A loud boat horn sounded several times.

Sandra said, "Sounds like someone is having a party. She must have docked next door, but I didn't know there was a place there for her to tie up."

They couldn't see anything through the trees beyond the fence at the marina property line. But as they watched, a German convertible sports car with two women inside came into view from behind the dry storage boat storage barn. It pulled up to an electric gate in the fence that opened quickly. The car disappeared past the tree line after they drove through, and the gate closed back behind them.

The Mole said, "The next time I see Murphy, I'm going to ask him what he knows about that place. I wonder if it's part of *Mallard Cove*."

"I'm guessing it is since the gate opens from here into there." Sandra was as intrigued as her father.

"Well, if it's another part of the marina that's more private, he should've told us about it. He knew that privacy was what I was after." The Mole was irritated by what he perceived as a slight.

"But if it is a party, depending on what goes on over there, it might not be someplace you would want to be connected with. How about letting me talk to Murphy?"

The Mole thought it over for a few seconds. "That might be better. No sense in my getting into an argument over it with him, and I could see that he was happier talking with you."

She smiled, "I'll take care of it."

He nodded. "Is Marty staying aboard tonight?"

"No. He said he would board before we leave in the morning. You know how he feels about the boat."

"Yes, he's made that quite clear. He's made several more things clear as well, mostly about how he doesn't agree with me about certain things. And that list is getting longer." He paused a minute before adding, "Actually, he doesn't agree with *us*. That's partly why I want to keep expanding your public role. I'm not going to put up with any bickering out in the open from him.

"I know he thinks that he could've created this ministry from the ground up all by himself and that it's his birthright. But I know that if it wasn't for you coming along, he would run it back into the ground if it was left only to him. And it's far from any birthright of his. You've done so much more to earn it, and to help me build it."

"I've been happy to. And I'll gladly do whatever you need me to keep expanding it."

"Yes. A big part of that is going to be managing your brother. And unfortunately, I think that'll be a continually growing part of your duties. He's getting tougher to handle. If it were up to him, I think he'd have us going back to only doing tent revivals and dropping the mystical water, the prayer cubes, and anything to do with the internet.

"But he'd probably still want his grand vacations and private jet rides, all while moving away from the prosperity gospel. He wasn't there with your grandparents like I was, scraping to get by, depending on the meager take from when we passed the plate every night. It wasn't until I got them to accept the true meaning of the gospel toward the end of their lives that our family had anything approaching stability and security. He doesn't appreciate what is right there in front of him. Like you do."

He smiled at his daughter, and she reached over and lightly gripped his arm while returning the smile. She did appreciate the ministry that he had built and understood exactly what it was. But she could also see what she could make it, so long as her brother didn't interfere.

10

REV'D UP REBOUND

"Want to fish in the morning?" I asked Casey as we sat on chairs around the fire pit next to his open-air outdoor kitchen.

"It *is* morning," he replied.

I looked at my watch and saw he was right. It had been morning for almost half an hour. He and I were the last ones here at C2, most having left over an hour ago. Lindsay and Dawn went over to our warm houseboat for a nightcap after we finished cleaning up. But despite the dropping temperature Case and I opted instead for one last beer each in front of the fire, which was slowly dying.

"Okay, then do you want to go fishing after daylight?"

"How much after daylight?" He asked.

"Long enough to get six hours of shuteye, and breakfast of some kind after daylight."

"Your boat or mine?"

"My Merritt. Fall west wind supposed to be starting up around noon, and I figured we'd run up around Reedville, and see if we can find some rockfish for dinner."

"Bring the girls?" He asked.

"We'd be dead meat if we didn't. In fact, how about inviting Eric, Candi, and Missy? We can pick them up on the way."

"Done deal. I'll email him so he gets it in the morning when he wakes up. What about Sandy?"

"Oh sure," I said. "Might as well throw gasoline on the fire."

"He's getting ready to head south, I'd love to spend another day with him before he goes."

"True. Then even if we don't catch anything, it won't be boring."

EARLY THE NEXT MORNING, Branson turned on the television to catch the repeat of their show from last night. What he saw instead made him blow a gasket. The Mole and his two kids were hawking a new product in an advertising spot during their show! The thing was a "prayer cube," some kind of audio player with hours of his voice, repeating Scripture and Bible verses. Branson reached for his phone to call Keller, not caring that the sun had barely risen. This had to be stopped, and *now*.

LINDSAY, Dawn, Casey, and I were seated on the patio at the *Cove*, finishing up our breakfast. It had been a great party the night before, and since it had been beer and wine only with piles of food, nobody was that much the worse for wear. Casey and Dawn had given most of their crew time off after the long trip, including their chef. And this morning none of us wanted to cook, so we had agreed to meet here to have breakfast before we left. A couple of the charter boats had already gone out, so our table had a great view straight down the basin through their empty slips. It was a cool and serene morning.

"About time youse guys showed up, we're burnin' daylight, and we've got a long run ahead of us!" Baloney was on the flybridge of *My Mahi*, lambasting a very tardy charter bunch that looked like they'd partied a bit too hearty last night. He preferred his charters to be early, and not hungover.

Oh, and Bill wasn't directly beside us, he was three slips over. What he lacked in height, he more than made up for in volume. The joke among the charter boats was that he didn't need a VHF radio; his voice had about the same range. If you could see him, no matter the distance, you could hear him.

As we watched his sport fisherman pull out of the slip, Casey remarked, "It was a great trip, but how good it is to be home. I didn't realize it until just now, but I've missed Baloney yelling at late charters."

We all laughed, but it was true. Baloney's bellowing, along with his antics, was part of what made *Mallard Cove* unique and special. And speaking of his antics, he was extra irritated with his charter today. We could tell by the puffs of smoke coming from the flybridge even before he made his turn to go out the basin's inlet. He had lit his noxious cigar early, breaking the rules no doubt so the smoke could drift down into the cockpit and reach the already ailing members of his charter. Once he sped up to cruising speed out beyond the breakwater, the full effect of the offensive stogie would be lost in the breeze until they slowed down to fish.

Down at the farthest large dock, I saw that *Privacy* was pulling away from the "tee" at the end.

"Well? Are you all staying up there until they start serving lunch, or are we going to get a move on?" Sandy had arrived at the bottom of the patio deck's stairs. He had wanted to get in a couple of hours of writing before we left, so he'd gotten up extra early this morning.

"We just got our coffees refilled. Come up and have one," Casey said.

Begrudgingly, he mounted the steps and pulled a chair up to the corner of our table between Lindsay and Dawn. "If I'd have known you were going to sit around all morning, I'd have written another book or two while I waited," he grumped.

"Take a chill pill and relax," I said. "We'll go in a minute. We can only keep one rockfish each per day this year anyway, so there's no hurry."

"We're running over to Reedville just for one rock apiece?"

"Hey, it beats you sitting at the dock all day pounding away at a keyboard, doesn't it? You can do that on the way down to Florida while Micah runs the boat if you want. Besides, you love our company."

He snorted. "The company of your women, yes. With you two, the jury is still out about that. By the way, you *did* put plenty of beer on the boat, right? If you're going to keep me away from my writing, the least you can do is support my beer habit."

"Two cases of Jamaican Red Stripe. Happy now?" I ribbed him.

"Red Stripe, eh? Good brand. Hey, you're rubbing off on the boy, Casey. He needs to hang around you more."

I said, "Well, I almost got a cheaper brand just to annoy you, but then you'd annoy me...all day."

He shot me an irritated look. "Damn right I would've."

Lindsay reached over and patted him on the arm, "I'm glad you're going with us today, Sandy. It's been fun having you here in the little cove this summer. We're going to miss you until you get back next spring."

He couldn't have brightened up more if I'd put ten cases of Red Stripe on *his* boat. "Well, that goes both ways. And I'm sorry ladies that I won't be here to help you keep these two in line this winter." He motioned to Casey and me. "Oh, and Gilligan, too. I see he's out torturing another poor charter group this morning."

Dawn said, "We heard him leave a little while ago."

Sandy snorted. "Heard his boat, or him?"

She replied, "Yes."

We all laughed, but I knew that Sandy and Bill would miss their sparring this winter. Those two won't admit it, but they've become good friends. And the next few weeks were going to bring a lot of changes when Sandy leaves, as the days grow colder and shorter, and the northern tuna boats arrive with their crews for the filming of another season of *Tuna Hunters*. When that happens, we'll barely see

Baloney until sometime after the first of the year. So, I'm really glad that Sandy is spending the day with us.

I looked over at the basin and saw something I thought and hoped I wouldn't, ever again. *Rev'd Up* was coming in through the inlet, and it looked like Keller and Branson were aboard. They looked over toward Privacy's dock, then spun around and left, somehow managing to miss all the docks, rocks, and boats. I wonder what the heck they are up to.

KELLER PULLED in through the *Mallard Cove* inlet, then looked east. The dock "tee" that had previously held *Privacy* was empty.

"Where is it!" Branson exploded.

"He left already. But he said he was planning a cruise to *Bayside* today."

"You know where that is?"

Keller nodded. "And I know what course they'll be steering."

He was still upset that the Mole was ignoring his calls, necessitating this morning's trip across the mouth of the Chesapeake. Now it looked like the trip was about to get even longer.

FISHING HAS ALWAYS BEEN fun for me, but it's even more so now that I don't have to do it to make a living. I can finally pick and choose not only when I want to fish, but who I want to fish with. Of course, today's group is made up of many of my favorites, and the five of us were seated around the flybridge of my Merritt.

Eric had texted Casey early this morning that he and Missy would love to go, but Candi had a date with the spa. So, after we cleared Fisherman Inlet Bridge, we made our turn to the north, heading for *Bayside* to pick up the two of them. Off in the distance toward the middle of the bay, I spotted a familiar light green hull. I picked up the VHF mic.

"*My Mahi, Irish Luck.* Ya on, Bill?"

"I gotcha good, go ahead, Murph."

"Any luck?"

"Not yet. But one of my charter just started 'chumming,' so maybe that'll help." He laughed, "Case of the ol' rum flu."

I looked at the water, which had only little two-foot-long rollers. That guy had better pray it's not a full-day charter, because, by the end of the day when both the wind and the waves pick up, he's going to want to die.

Sandy grabbed the mic. "Hey, Gilligan! If you'd quit smoking those old rubber tires, your charters might manage to live through a trip!"

"I told you to quit callin' me that! And if you don't write another book soon, I'm gonna run out of toilet paper!"

I wrestled the mic back from Sandy. "Okay, Bill, if you get on 'em, give me a call on my cell." It may be starting to dawn on both of them just how much they'll miss each other this winter.

"You, too. *My Mahi,* over and out."

Not thirty seconds later I hear Jimbo Morris chime in, "Hey Gilligan, I'm on 'em over here." He runs an old forty-six-foot Bertram out of Deltaville and is part of the southern contingent of *Tuna Hunters.*

"Damn it, not you too, Jimbo. Sandy, I'll get you for this!"

Sandy reached for the mic again, but I blocked him this time. But I couldn't block that self-satisfied grin he was wearing. Then again, we all were smiling at Bill's now locally famous second nickname.

"He's never going to live that down," Casey said.

Sandy grinned, "It'll give the old codger something to remind him of me until I get back."

"Jimbo will make sure of that," I chuckled. Then something about half a mile or so dead ahead caught my attention. It looked like *Privacy* was running at wide-open-throttle, throwing a huge wake, and a large center console was trying to lay up alongside her as they were running. That boat looked like Keller's. The bigger boat was zigging and zagging, trying to shake them. Lindsay saw me stare and quickly focused on the scene herself.

"Is that guy crazy? It looks like someone's trying to board her!"

Now all of us were watching this unfold. As much as I disliked the Mole, I disliked Keller even more. And I can rank my priorities, starting with the fact that I've made money off the Mole. I grabbed both throttles and "firewalled" them. *Irish Luck*'s twin ten-cylinder Man diesels instantly responded, taking her up to her top speed of thirty-two knots, or about thirty-seven miles per hour. I switched the VHF over from the fishing channel to a hailing frequency.

"Motoryacht *Privacy*, *Irish Luck*. Are you on, Gary?"

"Yeah, Murph, go up two and drop to low power."

I turned to a channel two above the hailing one and switched to low power mode so my transmissions wouldn't travel far.

"Hey Murph, you here?" Since I had sold the Westport to Stoneman and he'd kept the crew on, I knew the captain, Gary Stevens. Good guy, with a great reputation.

"Yeah. What's going on over there? I'm on your starboard, aft about a quarter-mile."

"Two crazies that the boss has had bad dealings with have been trying to get me to stop so they can board us."

I asked, "Have you called the Coasties?"

"Negative. The boss doesn't want the publicity and wants me to try to shake 'em. We've bumped a couple of times, and I think the bigger guy is still gonna try to board us, even at this speed."

"Okay, Gary, I've got an idea. You ever go tubing behind an outboard?"

"Sure?"

I said, "We're gonna pull alongside and 'bull ring' this idiot, but in a straight line and sandwich him."

We could hear the relief in his voice. "Gotcha. I'll hold the helm straight when you're abeam of me."

At wide-open-throttle, the Westport's top speed is twenty-six knots or thirty miles per hour. At this speed, the massive boat throws a huge wake from both the bow and the stern. As the bow carves through the water like a knife, it throws off what surfers would describe as a "tube" about five feet high and extending back almost thirty feet. The tube, and the combined spray and wake where it lands back on the water's surface, extends out about twenty feet on either side of the hull.

Keller was trying to get alongside the boat in the trough that's formed between the tube and the stern wake that starts two-thirds of the way back along the hull. This forty-foot section of water may look smooth to a boating newbie like Keller, but it's very turbulent under the surface. It's packed with a lot of energy, as the displaced water from under the hull is squeezed out to the side. Almost as much energy as the turbulence behind the stern that forms the big "rooster tail," which reaches about four feet high. Not surprising when you realize that her displacement is 275,000 pounds. Add this spray show to Gary's zigzagging, and it makes *Privacy* a very elusive target.

If you've never tried to transfer from one moving boat to another, that's good, don't ever do it. This is probably one of the most dangerous things that can be done around a moving vessel. I know, because I've done it. Because it was a matter of life and death with an out-of-control yacht, that's why! And I went from the bow of Casey's boat across the transom of the other boat with Casey at the controls of his, and Baloney calling distances from up on the bow with me. As much as we all kid him, I have as much respect for Bill's boating knowledge and skill as I do for Casey's, and that's saying a lot. But I successfully made the transfer, managing to get shot in the butt as thanks for my efforts, but this is all a story for another day. And I need to concentrate on catching up to Gary.

11

SHOOT THE "TUBE"

The Mole continued to ignore Keller's calls while they were underway, unaware that they were being pursued by both Branson and him. From up on his flybridge deck he spotted the center console when it was about a half-mile back and closing rapidly, making a beeline straight for them. Looking through a set of binoculars, he recognized both occupants. He told his captain to go to full speed and avoid the boat, but to keep radio silence if they tried to hail them. He had briefly considered bringing along some body-guards for the trip. But he had figured that no one would try anything out here on the bay, and *Bayside* is known for having very tight secu-rity for their guests.

"Get up alongside, and motion for 'em to shut down," Branson directed.

Keller did as he was told, pulling up even with the flying bridge, but outside of the yacht's bow wake. And despite getting both the yacht's captain and the Mole's attention at first, they were ignoring him now. Branson began screaming at the Mole to shut down so they could talk, but instead, he disappeared down into the cabin.

"Get me over there to their swim platform, I'll climb aboard."

Keller recoiled, "Are you crazy? There's no way I can get near that with their wake!"

"Fine, then get me up to the middle of this side, where they put that ramp thing down at the dock. I'm not gonna let this jerk get away with ignoring me and selling us a bill of goods while laughing at us by putting his ads on our show! There, get me to those stainless pipe things so I can grab onto 'em." He pointed to the stainless railings that flanked the gangway opening, about nine feet above the water.

"I'll try, but if you fall, you'll either end up in my props or theirs."

Branson glared at him, "You just do a good job getting me next to them, and I won't!"

As they got closer to the yacht, Keller slowed to match its speed with one hand on his throttles and his other in a white-knuckled grip on the steering wheel. He managed to squeeze into the foamy surface between the bow and stern wakes but found that it wasn't as smooth in there as it looked; he had hit the unseen turbulence under the surface and had to fight to keep control of his boat. Branson climbed up onto the covering board on top of the gunwale and steadied himself with one hand on the edge of the hardtop as he prepared to make his transfer.

Suddenly the yacht turned hard to the right, and Keller didn't react fast enough. *Rev'd Up* hit *Privacy* and violently ricocheted off her hull and into the residual turbulence from the bow wake.

"What the hell are you doing, Keller? I almost went over the side!" Branson was furious, having fallen to their deck. For a split second, Keller wished that he had.

"I warned you about their wake. That captain is crazy! I can't get you near enough if he's going to keep maneuvering like that."

Branson pulled himself back up and grabbed Keller's shirt, shaking him.

"You can, and you will! I'm not getting beaten by that walking rodent. Now, get me back over there!"

Branson climbed back up on the gunwale, and this time he held the hardtop with both hands as Keller moved in cautiously. But Stevens saw him coming and again made another hard turn. Their collision this time wasn't as hard, but it was still unnerving. This dance continued for more than five minutes until the yacht went back to holding a straight course and it started to slow. Keller mistakenly thought that they were going to stop after all and throttled back to match his speed.

Almost anyone who has ever ridden an innertube towed behind an outboard knows about "bullrings." They are wakes created when the towboat goes around and around in a circle. Its inner wake eventually crashes into itself, creating a big "bullseye" looking wake in the center. While the towboat circles, the tube whips out beyond the outer wake. Then the driver widens the circle and turns back sharply, accelerating the tube like a pendulum and shooting it back through the "bullring" at high speed. Going through it with those waves crashing together in the middle is as rough as riding a rodeo bull, and often the result is that the tube and the rider become separated. The rider becomes airborne, crashing hard back into the water. We were about to make Keller that rider.

He was so intent on watching *Privacy* that he didn't see *Irish Luck* coming up to starboard, also slowing and now throwing the largest wake she could make. By the time he spotted her, the wakes from both boats were "zippering" closed together and already had him hemmed in as the Merritt moved over closer. Keller went for his throttles, hoping to get ahead of the two wake's convergence which had now formed its five-foot rooster tail, a straight-line "bullring" that was advancing toward him like a zipper closing. But with *Irish Luck* moving closer and closer to *Privacy*, Keller's only avenue of escape where he'd have any hope of keeping control was through the roughest, highest part of the bow wake, the tube.

"LINDS, start videoing this. I want to get them harassing Gary, show that was their intent, and that he was just trying to avoid them," I said.

"Got it!" She took out her phone.

"You're right, this is much better than staying at the dock." Sandy was grinning, probably already figuring out where he would put all this in his next book.

"Oh, it's about to get a lot better. We're going to go over and protect our friends," I said. Sandy gave me a questioning look when I said "friends," but I put a finger across my lips and pointed to Lindsay's phone, which was picking up everything that was said on the bridge. He nodded, understanding that this could end up getting used as evidence at some point if there was an official inquest.

I kept into the throttles until I was almost caught up to *Privacy* and saw that Gary had slowed slightly as he straightened his track. His speed was perfect. By slowing to match it, this allowed me to throw the Merritt's largest possible wake as my bow raised while the stern settled slightly. I was now inching my way up opposite *Rev'd Up* and over toward him. The combined wakes from the Westport and my Merritt were now creating a huge rooster tail that would prevent Keller from dropping back to get away. If that rooster's tail hits his boat, it could swamp him or make him lose control. But with my putting the squeeze on him from the side, his only option to escape was to try and power through *Privacy*'s bow wake, as I edged closer and closer over toward him. He was so intent on the yacht that he only spotted my bow when it was just twenty feet abeam. He glanced back and realized trying to escape that way wasn't an option, so he gunned it.

He misjudged how powerful the tube wake from Gary's bow was. It filled his boat with water, just as if a large, natural wave had broken over the boat. The added weight of all that water made the boat uncontrollable, and she started to broach, or make an uncontrolled turn at high speed. It's the nautical equivalent of an aircraft hitting a wing on the ground and causing it to ground loop.

Anticipating this, I peeled off, and he narrowly missed my stern but caught the full brunt of first my wake, and then Gary's. How he kept from rolling over with all that water's weight in his boat I have no idea. But he heeled over far enough that one covering board went all the way underwater before the boat slowly righted itself, inches from being completely swamped. For his sake, I hope he had a spare pair of underwear onboard; that was one hairy ride.

I again moved back to flank Gary, and I watched through binoculars as Keller opened the side door on his hull to try and save his boat. Normally that door is used for swimming, diving, or even pulling big fish in. But today, it became a giant scupper as it allowed the water that had nearly sunk him to escape. The self-bailing deck's regular scuppers couldn't come close to handling it all. The boat's painted waterline finally reappeared after literally tons of water flowed out through the side. As it was, she'd taken some water in around the console hatch and the one in the cuddy cabin up forward, and Keller's pumps were working hard to drain those sections of the bilge.

For the second time in two months, I left this jerk to fend for himself after he did something stupid out on the water. That's a new record for me. But he's lucky I don't feel like going back around to sink him, and that I'd rather go fishing with my friends. And at the rate he's going he'll end up as a "Darwin Award" recipient sooner or later, anyway.

"Do something, Keller!" Branson jumped back onto the deck after spotting the big sportfish and the waves approaching.

Keller didn't say a word as he shoved the throttles forward to try to get away. He had no choice but to head into the massive bow spray and the giant water tube. He hadn't imagined the huge amount of water that was being displaced and forced away from the yacht's bow, but a large percentage of it was now dumping into the cockpit of his boat. And if the weight of the water wasn't enough, it felt like a giant's hand was now shoving his hull sideways. He was forced away from the yacht and into the path of the sportfishing boat, which could easily cut his boat in two if it hit him.

Fortunately, whoever was operating it had anticipated what might happen and had veered off as the center console suddenly slowed, then violently and uncontrollably turned to the right. Then the wakes from the other boats slammed into the foundering craft. Both men held on for dear life as the boat heeled over, water now pouring over the one gunwale and almost completely filling the interior. One of the motors screamed as it came out of the water and briefly over-revved. Keller yanked the throttles back into neutral as the boat ceased its roll, slowly righting itself. The whole thing seemed to happen in slow motion, taking minutes, but in reality, it was over in mere seconds. Branson was screaming, "Kelllllerrr!" but by then the worst was over, though the swamped boat remained very unstable.

"Branson don't move! We could still roll over." Even as inexperienced as he was, Keller knew that he had to get the water out of the boat, and fast. He had a sudden thought and slowly, very carefully, he made his way over to the gunwale door. Undoing the latches, he swung the covering board section up, and the actual door outward. The air trapped in the inner hull below the cockpit deck gave it enough buoyancy to start pushing the water out. Within two minutes the deck was again above the water, and the bilge pumps were taking care of what had leaked below.

Now that the worst was over, Keller realized that he had seen something in Branson that he never had before. Fear. But as swiftly as it had come, it disappeared.

"You almost killed us!" Branson yelled as he advanced toward Keller. But this time instead of cowering, Keller held his ground.

"I almost killed us," Keller asked incredulously. "YOU were the one that insisted you board that boat while it was running! I didn't want to go near it! If you hadn't been so bone-headed, we'd have never ended up in their wake!"

Instead of replying, Branson swung at Keller, who then ducked. His fist connected with one of the anodized aluminum pipe supports of the hardtop and Branson screamed again. Pulling his hand back he could see that two of his knuckles weren't where they should be, instead, they were indented, sunken back onto his hand which was rapidly swelling and turning blue. He grabbed it with his other hand to support the two fingers the knuckles were attached to.

"It's broke, I need a doctor!"

Keller replied, "Yeah, a psychiatrist."

"Get me the hell back to Virginia Beach, and now! I need to go to the hospital."

Keller realized that he'd have been the one who needed the hospital if Branson had connected with his face instead of the support. "Yeah, well, go sit in the bow and I'll get us back there."

He cranked the engines as Branson got situated in a seat up forward. He set a course for Virginia Beach, but only took her up to a slow cruising speed. More time to look for some rough waves to hit as hard as possible to make Branson's trip an agonizing one. He smiled to himself as he leaned back against his seat.

Lindsay had taken the glasses from me, as I now concentrated on running the boat. The VHF squawked, "Thank you, Murph, I owe you, big time! I bet he doesn't try that crap again anytime soon."

"The craziest thing I've seen on the water in quite a while, and that's saying something, Gary. And I'll settle for a drink at the *Beach Bar* when you get back."

"Roger that, Cap. You're on, but for more than just one, I've got your whole bar tab!"

Lindsay interrupted our conversation, still looking through the binoculars.

"Oh, it just got crazier; those two are fighting. Wait, the fight's over. The big guy missed and hit a top support. The way he's holding his hand, it looks like he may have broken something."

Sandy piped up, "This day just keeps getting better and better! And I thought that you two were good for stories, Casey and Dawn.

But I've hit the jackpot with these two kids. I need to hang around you guys more often when I get back."

"Bring your own beer," I said.

"Ours too," Linds added.

"Huh? What? Oh, haha. Funny people."

The other four of us laughed, it was a good release for the tension that had been built up by what had happened.

Linds took another look through the glasses, "Looks like they've had enough. They're hooked up and headed back south."

I looked over and waved at Gary, which he returned as I slowly eased my throttles forward, bringing us back up to a high cruising speed. As I resumed our course for *Bayside*, I saw Casey was on the phone.

After Casey hung up, he said, "I've arranged with Rik for some extra security for the Mole through his stay at *Bayside*. We don't need any negative publicity if those guys show up and they all get into it there. We're going to make sure that Keller and his bunch aren't allowed anywhere near the place."

This is part of why I love being in partnership with Casey; it's all about the details with him. I nodded and leaned back in my helm seat, wondering if I hadn't known the crew, would I have jumped in the middle of that incident? I'd like to think I would always come to the rescue of anyone being attacked out on the water, but when it came to the Mole, I wasn't too sure of that.

"You see, father? THIS is what comes of your beliefs! It's what happens when enough is never enough. You make enemies along the way, and they are only going to become more violent." Martin Junior was beside himself, finally speaking out against what he was finally seeing as a perversion of Scripture. Standing in front of what had become his father's chair in the salon of the yacht, he stared down at him as the Mole met his eyes with a steely look.

"And *you* see that He protected us, Martin. Because we are

following the path that He laid out in front of us. Do you think that Murphy just happened to come along? You say that you too have the gift, yet it looks like you are still blind." The Mole sounded as sad as he felt.

"You can't twist things around just to support your narrative, father! We need to go back to what your father preached, the real gospel as it was written and intended. The TRUE meaning. Your father never needed bodyguards, or to be walled off from the people who he was trying to save!"

The Mole became angry. "You weren't there, Junior, I was! Traveling from place to place with barely enough money for gas, much less for food. Being dependent on the generosity of the flock, not knowing where our next meal was coming from, much less what it would be.

"Have you ever tasted squirrel, Junior, much less made a meal out of it? No, but I have! You've always had nothing but the best from the day that you were born, and it was because of the prosperity gospel. Look around you right now, my parents never dreamed of luxury like this, never saw any vessel so splendid. Not even as a guest, much less as an owner! And toward the end of their lives, I was finally able to get them to see the wisdom of the prosperity gospel."

Martin Junior was disgusted. "What has become of your faith? We're supposed to be in the business of saving souls."

The Mole jumped to his feet, coming face to face with his son. "That's exactly what we do! We save them from themselves. We give hope to those who have none, so they believe they can finally reach their full potential! Without hope, Junior, nothing is possible. And that's the faith I have! My only regret is that your mother didn't live long enough to see the size of the ministry that we've built." His eyes almost glowed with the fire of his determination.

Sandra forced her way between them, pushing her brother back. "Enough, both of you! Bickering like this isn't going to lead anywhere! Marty, you need to go cool off and pray for direction. And father, you need to calm down. You know this is the worst thing for your blood pressure. Sit down, and I'll get you more tea."

"What, now you are going to start telling both of us what to do, sis? Step up now and shove both of us around?" Marty demanded.

"If that's what it takes to hold this family and our ministry together, then yes, that's exactly what I'll do! There's a hundred and twelve feet of this yacht and plenty of places for you to go cool off while you leave father to do the same. So, go!"

"I will, but not because you told me to, but because I was going to anyway." He stormed off and out the side salon door.

Martin Stoneman smiled at his daughter. Stepping up and in as she had was exactly what he was hoping to see from her for all these years. He realized that she is now as able to lead their ministry and preach as any man would be, especially Marty. His son had now become a major disappointment, questioning the very tenets of their belief.

He watched as Sandra went to the galley to bring him more of his special tea. He knew then that Marty would have to be out, and that she would be the next leader of their church.

12

CAPTAIN MISSY

Pulling into the marina at *Bayside,* I flashed back to the first time I saw the property a few years ago. What a difference a few years, a pile of cash and a big dose of Casey Shaw's vision can make to a place. It was now the gem of the Chesapeake with its boutique hotel, private club, and spa, as well as an exclusive housing development. Casey and Dawn had lived here from that first day until he ran into some trouble a while back. While that was nothing of his own doing, the two of them decided it was in the best interest of the partnership's investment if they were to leave.

Frankly, they both were tired of living more or less in a fishbowl here anyway, and when Casey stumbled on the *C2* property next to *Mallard Cove,* he knew it was the perfect solution for them as well as the rest of us. He had gone from semi-famous to downright infamous, and you'll never know just how valuable your privacy is until it's gone. So, while he was vindicated in the end with his integrity restored, the mud always gets put on the front page, and any retraction is usually small and on the back pages, like it was in his case. He's enjoying his lower profile at *Mallard Cove* these days.

I pulled us up to a "tee" at the end of a dock on the north side, across the basin from Eric's vintage seventy-five-foot Trumpy yacht,

MissE. Since we wouldn't be here long, Lindsay only secured us with a single line from the spring cleat to the floating dock. Rikki was already waiting there for us, alerted by Casey's call. Behind her, Missy and Eric were just walking up. They listened as Casey and Rik conferred, then the three of them boarded as Rik waved goodbye. She went toward the nondescript office building across the hotel's driveway that *ESVA Security* shares with *Bayside Management.*

I looked down into the cockpit, "Hey, Missy, can you come up here?"

She climbed the ladder with an inquisitive look on her face. I motioned to the wheel.

"Can't catch any fish in here. Take us out."

She beamed, "Me?"

"Why not? You've seen both Casey and me do it countless times, and you've been running your outboard for over a year now. You've got this. Back us off the dock, then use one gear in forward and one in reverse to pivot us until we're almost facing out the inlet, then put the other in forward gear. Don't get into the throttles unless you have to. And whatever you do, don't hit that Trumpy. The owner's a real grump."

She laughed at the Trumpy reference to her father, then turned serious.

"Got it! But don't go anywhere."

"I'll be right here if you need me, but you won't."

Now it was my turn to grin because there's nothing like watching the thrill and intensity of a teenager taking a large boat out for the first time. I looked over at Sandy, who winked at me. We all liked Missy, whose real name was Elaina, which is where both "*MissE*" and "Missy" came from.

I sat in an identical seat beside the varnished helm chair. Both were mounted on pedestals. Normally they face the bow, or you can swivel them all the way around, facing the fishing cockpit below. But Missy wasn't sitting in the chair, she was standing in front of it, facing backward with her butt against the wheel. Her hands were on each gear/throttle on either side of the helm pod. This is the proper and professional way to back a boat, facing aft so you have the full view of where you are going, instead of having to look back over your shoulder.

Missy put the port gear in reverse, then as the stern started to kick out away from the dock, she matched the starboard with it. Once out toward the middle between two docks, she put the starboard in forward. When you maneuver in close like this, you only use your gears. The rudders are ineffective unless they have a lot of water running past them, but the props can push hard in one direction or the other from a dead stop.

As the boat started to pivot and was no longer backing up, Missy turned around and faced forward, being careful not to hit anything with the long bow, *especially* her dad's Trumpy. And just as I told her, she put the port transmission in forward gear when we were almost lined up with the inlet. The momentum from the pivot kept the bow moving sideways until enough water was now going across the rudders, and she started controlling the boat with the steering wheel from that point on.

"How'd she do?" Lindsay was climbing up the ladder with three coat bags. Eric, Casey, and Dawn followed her up.

"Handled it like a pro," I replied.

"So, she qualifies?" Linds was grinning.

"She does."

Missy said, "Wait, what did I qualify for?"

"This!" Linds unzipped the coat bag and removed a lined crew jacket embroidered with *"Missy"* on one side of the front, and *"Mallard Cove Women's Fishing Team"* on the other. "I mean if you want to team up with Dawn, Kari, and me."

"Heck, yes! That is so cool, thank you! Does this mean we're going to fish tournaments?"

"That's exactly what it means." She unbagged a jacket for herself and one for Dawn, as Missy exchanged the jacket she was wearing for the new one.

"But today, you're going to find us some rockfish over by Reedville," I said.

"I'm running the boat?"

"Yep. If you want to fish tournaments, you need to be able to do everything on the boat, including finding us some fish. Let's go!"

She brought us up to cruising speed and turned in the direction of Reedville, on the other side of the bay. We passed *Privacy* on our way out, and Gary blew a long blast on his horn. We all waved in reply, and fortunately, there was no sign of Keller and company behind him.

TWO HOURS later we all had our daily quota of one rockfish each. I had taken the wheel only long enough for Missy to catch hers, and she was now back at the helm.

I said, "Head for the Piankatank River, south of Deltaville. We'll duck in behind Gwynn's Island and grab some lunch over there."

Casey had just climbed the ladder to join us on the flybridge,

"Is this about lunch, or are you curious about that property we missed?"

"Yes," I replied. "But you'll see, lunch at *Bay Breeze* is tough to beat on this side of the bay."

ERIC, Casey, and I had all been working with Missy on her boating skills this past summer. She was a natural, having a real feel for running her outboard, an eighteen-foot custom Winter hull named *Lil' Miss*, a smaller version of Casey's *Incognito*. Fishing came naturally to her, and Eric wanted to be sure she was as safe out on the water as possible. Heck, we all did. So, we were trying to get her as much time in as many different boats as possible. She'd run Casey's fifty-five-foot Jarrett Bay sportfish when we were out fishing, as well as my Merritt, but only when we were away from the dock. It's why today is such a big deal. Maneuvering in the tight spaces of a marina can take some finesse. Some people just never get the hang of it and are "pinball wizards" like Keller. But Missy has the knack for it.

Like we all had been teaching her, she watched out ahead

underway as well as glanced occasionally at the GPS plotter I had pulled up on a flat panel display. As part of her training, I've been harping on how the majority of boaters these days would be lost if their electronics died. So, I also stressed for her to practice "dead reckoning," to make use of the good old standby magnetic compass without relying on the GPS. There are a lot of days out on the Chesapeake when fog rolls in, and if you don't have radar or a plotter, you better have a chart and a good compass if you want to get home.

We were all trying to make sure she'd be as safe alone out in her outboard as she is on one of our sportfish rigs with the rest of us. And the time we spent with her was paying off, just like it is today. I didn't have to say much, other than to point out exactly where our lunch stop was.

Missy slowed to idle speed as we approached the hotel property. Even from out in the channel Casey and I could see that they were only doing a superficial "rehab" of the property. For starters, we could see that they had just patched the roofs instead of replacing them. The sections with the new shingles stood out like an asphalt version of chicken pox. A small construction dumpster sat outside instead of the larger ones that should've been filled by now with carpet, along with plenty of drywall, and rotten wood. They were halfway finished repainting the exterior, but little or no prep work had been done. Their contractor was spraying over old, peeling paint, and mildew. The numerous potholes in the asphalt parking lot looked like they had been filled with bagged concrete.

If all that wasn't bad enough, they obviously knew nothing about running a marina. Some jackleg operation was in there with a tiny barge and a homemade gin pole, replacing pilings in the slips with the thinnest new pilings I'd seen in quite a while. And instead of widening and lengthening the slips, they were replacing the pilings in the same locations. This marina was built over sixty years ago when the average boat was much narrower and shorter than today. Then again, this work was on par with what was being done on the hotel.

Casey hadn't seen the place except for the pictures and video Kari had sent him on his honeymoon cruise, and in passing from the bridge road years ago.

"Damn. I can see why you wanted it, and now look at the crappy job they're doing with it."

Casey hates a "fluff job" in place of a proper renovation as much as I do. But having gone after this property with the disadvantage of being an honest, tax-paying organization, it stung to see it being so badly reworked by a group that had such an advantage over us.

I replied, "Yeah. This sucks, knowing what it could be not just for us, but for the people of the county, hauling in a lot of tax revenue. Seeing this, you know how it's going to be run. Talk about a lose/lose proposition for the area. I'm mad as hell, knowing that those jerks are as phony as the day is long, pretending to be something they aren't. I'd love to figure out a way to do something about it."

Casey said, "Let's both think that over. I sure don't want to lose any more deals to them because they have an unfair and illegal advantage. There has to be a way to put an end to it."

Sandy had been quietly listening to our conversation. "You know, sometimes you can use a person's strengths against them. Owning that show makes them a strong force that politicians don't want to mess with. Their audience is big, and they vote. But these guys have to be pretty leveraged to have bought it as well as a pile of real estate. If their audience were to see them as you have, seems to me they'd draw some quick conclusions about those not-so-holy-men."

"Good point, Sandy. Now, all we have to do is figure out how to accomplish that," Casey said.

"My money is on you boys. You'll figure a way."

Cindy and two of Rikki's associates met *Privacy* as they docked. The Mole was going to get his special treatment after all, though they are more interested in protecting *Bayside's* reputation than Stoneman.

Marty got off the boat, wanting to put some distance between himself, Sandra, and their father. A large section of the property is crisscrossed with nature trails, so he headed to the wilderness preserve to clear his head and think. The Mole went to the spa for a massage, and the start of his pampered weekend, while Sandra hit the hot tub and the heated pool. She needed the swim to relax after what should have been a relaxing inaugural trip, but that had quickly turned into the cruise from hell. She wanted to get the swim in before the weather turned.

After her swim she was finishing a late lunch when she spotted *Irish Luck* approaching from offshore, spray shooting out to the sides of her bow. The wind had picked up along with the waves, as gray clouds moved in ahead of the cold front. Sandra signed her check and rushed to the marina to meet the boat.

I saw there were no open dock "tees" in the marina, but there was an empty slip just inside of *Privacy*. Missy took all this in at the same time, then gave me a concerned look.

"What? You've got this! Take the empty one inside that Westport." I tilted my head slightly, returning my look of confidence and challenge. Her face quickly mirrored mine as she pulled in between the two long docks, stopped, and backed into the slip executing a perfect backward ninety-degree turn as she did. *Irish Luck* laid up perfectly, stern-first, next to the inside of the "tee," and I have to say, I couldn't have done it any better. I'm proud of my protégé, but not as proud as her dad, who had watched her from the cockpit.

Lindsay again secured us to the dock with a single spring line, anticipating a quick departure. Missy gave me a proud and happy hug, then went down the ladder. That's when I spotted Sandra Stoneman, walking out on the dock while looking up at me.

"Murph, would you mind if I came aboard to talk to you for a minute?"

"I'll be right down."

She shook her head, "No, stay put, I'll come up there."

She passed most of our party down in the cockpit as she made her way to the ladder. They weren't the only ones who wondered who she was, as Lindsay stepped from the dock to the covering board into the cockpit, carefully watching Sandra climb. As Sandra reached the bridge, I stuck my hand out, but she bypassed it to hug me. Over her shoulder, I saw Linds start moving toward the ladder.

Sandra backed up but kept her hands on my biceps. "Murph, I can't thank you enough for coming to our rescue this morning! I knew that Branson had a temper, but I never realized he was that crazy and dangerous."

"Miss Stoneman..."

"Sandra, please." She smiled.

"Sandra, your father is a customer, a good customer, and I wasn't about to stand by and let him get attacked, especially by Keller, with whom I had a score to settle myself. Casey, Dawn, and Eric..." I motioned to them in the cockpit, "...own the majority of *Bayside,* and are my partners in *Mallard Cove* as well, and they have arranged for some extra security for you while you're here."

"*Our* partners." Lindsay had reached the bridge deck, and like me, she had stuck out her hand, only hers was more intended for Sandra to let go of my arm than to "make nice."

"Hi, I'm Lindsay Davis, Murph's fiancée, and business partner."

Sandra let Lind's hand hang in the air for a spilled second too long and the temperature on the flybridge seemed to drop several degrees instantly. Sandra's head tilted slightly in acknowledgment as she shook hands and finally dropped her left hand off my other arm. This was almost as flattering as it was awkward as hell. Yet Sandra didn't seem to be embarrassed or put off.

"Very nice to meet you, Lindsay. I was just thanking Murph for coming to our rescue this morning, and I'd like to thank you as well. I'd love to have you both over to dinner on *Privacy* after we get back to *Mallard Cove.* How about Tuesday evening?"

I was trying to quickly come up with an excuse for getting out of it when Lindsay said, "We'd love to."

It was all I could do to keep my jaw from dropping, but then I saw *the* face. The one Lindsay gets when she's squaring off against an adversary. The one she had on right before hurling that sinker at

"Birddog" Cetta. It says that she's not about to back down or run. I had to do something to diffuse things fast.

"That'd be great, Sandra, thanks. What time?" I asked.

She turned back to me. "Six-thirty?"

Lindsay said firmly, "We'll be there."

Sandra smiled at me, nodded to Linds, then went down the ladder. That's when I noticed all our friends had been watching us while sitting on the stern's covering board like it was front-row seating at a prizefight. Sandy had a happy grin like he had just finished writing yet another chapter in his latest book. Sandra seemed not to notice the stares. She went over and introduced herself to everyone before climbing up onto the dock, then walking up *Privacy*'s gangway, glancing back over at me as she did.

Without saying a word, Lindsay went down the ladder. She'd caught that last look. After Eric and Missy climbed up onto the dock, she quickly uncleated the spring line.

"Let's go!"

Her voice wasn't happy, and I wondered what I had done wrong. It wasn't like I had encouraged Sandra to hug me, or even for her to climb up to the flybridge. There were a lot of things I learned about women during my time as a "player" in South Florida, but this kind of stuff wasn't part of that education. And people wonder why I never settled down before now.

Dawn climbed up first, shaking her head at me as she passed.

I said, "What?!?"

"You are so clueless."

"Ordinarily I'd argue about that, but in this case, I won't."

"Good idea on the second part. The first part just goes to show how clueless you are. But I think Linds will explain it to you in detail later."

"I have a bad feeling that you're right."

"Hey, you may be learning faster than I thought."

13

SAGE ADVICE

On the way back to *Mallard Cove*, Lindsay and Dawn sat on one side of the bridge while Sandy and Casey were on the other. I couldn't hear what the women were saying, but I could see Lindsay's face, and she wasn't happy. On the other side of the bridge, I easily overheard Casey giving Sandy the rundown on Ocracoke Island in North Carolina. It's an island at the end of the Outer Banks chain, just below Hatteras. It was also one of the favorite haunts of Edward Teach, also known as the pirate Blackbeard. Teach and Casey had that in common; Casey loves the place. Just off the south side of the island is where Teach met his fate, ambushed by a mercenary force sent by the governor of Virginia. The island was later purchased by Blackbeard's retired quartermaster.

Casey said, "It's one of my favorite islands, and reminds you of old Key West from so many years ago before the cruise ships started stopping there. I've got a lot of friends on the island including one who owns a restaurant that serves some of the best burgers on the planet. She's also a descendant of that quartermaster."

Sandy remarked, "Best burgers? This, coming from a guy that owns restaurants. That's high praise."

"And no exaggeration, Sandy. Another friend, Rita, runs Ocracats, a group that helps control the island's feral cat population." Casey knew that Sandy has a soft spot when it comes to animals.

"You don't mean…"

Casey said, "What? No! They have a spay and neuter clinic a couple of times a year, then they re-release and feed the adult cats that live in the marsh. Plus, they round up the feral kittens and get them out of the marsh and find homes for them, mostly off-island."

"Nice! I like it when people take matters into their own hands instead of waiting for the government to do it. It kind of sounds like what's about to happen to Murph. Getting neutered, then kicked out into the marsh." He looked at me and grinned.

I scowled back at Sandy, but Casey chuckled, glancing over at Lindsay to make certain she hadn't picked up on that before continuing. "Some people believe that the first pair of cats were brought to the island by Blackbeard, to cut down on the rat population. True story or not, it worked. You never see any rodents, unlike on other barrier islands. Oh, and another thing you won't see there are any stores or restaurants that are part of a chain. Everything is owned and run by independents."

"Again, sounds like my kind of place."

"That's why I brought it up. Good stop on your trip. Might also work as a book location."

"We'll overnight there on the way down."

Great, those two have now set Sandy's travel itinerary, but I was worried about what Dawn and Lindsay were planning. They were deliberately keeping their voices low, so something was up, and I'm sure I'll find out later what that something is. Which is the scary part.

MARTY WATCHED from the seawall as his sister threw herself on that Murphy guy, and he was disgusted. First, she jumps in between his father and him, and now she grabs onto this guy like some modern-day Jezebel. He saw it all as further evidence of his family's corruption by this so-called prosperity interpretation of the gospel. It was going to be up to him to make the two of them see the truth, that they are being co-opted by dark forces which are pulling them away from the one true God. They had already been betrayed by some that were thought to be loyal and faithful. Again, this was more evidence of the power of the sinister force aligned against them. Against him. And he wasn't about to stand by and watch his own family continue to besmirch and destroy their ministry. *His* ministry. This was his new life's mission, to carry on what his grandfather had started, preaching the same way that he had, and using that same gospel, not his father's perverted one. There was far too much work left to be done in this world, and he wasn't about to let his father and sister besmirch the family name any further and keep him from doing that work. Certainly not so they could sell trinkets and snake oil.

I SAID, "I don't get why you're upset."

Lindsay and I were back on *OCT* at the small cove after cleaning our fish and washing *Irish Luck*.

"Well, when your 'lunch buddy' turns out not to be some homely spinster-looking preacher woman but instead is halfway to hot, and *very* friendly, did you expect that I'd be happy about it? It makes me wonder what the two of you chatted about the other day."

"I never said she was 'spinster looking!' And it wasn't like we had a private conversation; her father and brother were both right there."

"But you never mentioned that she was pretty, either."

"I didn't think that it was that important! It wasn't like I went over there looking for a date, I was because the Mole ambushed me. Hell, I didn't even know that she and her brother were going to be there. If you'll remember, the Mole was just trying to get *Bayside* favors out of me, and to use me to throw Keller and his bunch off balance."

"It looked like she had another use for you on her mind."

"She's a minister!" I had no idea where this was coming from. Yes, Sandra is pretty. And a few years ago, I wouldn't have cared if she was the Archbishop of ESVA, I'd have loved to have gotten her out of her vestments. But I wasn't like that anymore. Ever since I'd met Lindsay, she was who I wanted. Period.

"Rev is a minister, too, but you said he's up for dating."

"Well, there's dating, and then there's *dating*. I'm not sure which type he's up for," I said.

"He's a guy, so I can tell you which type." She scowled at me like I should know this.

I almost jumped on her blanket condemnation of us males, but I could tell there was something behind this, something I wasn't picking up on. Lindsay is rarely moody and spoiling for a fight like she is now. But on those rare occasions when she was, I've found that the best thing to do is to give her space and let her cool off.

"You know, I think I'm going to go up to C2 and mix myself a drink and play a game or two of pool by myself."

"Yeah, well, do whatever you want, you're going to anyway."

I probably gave her an astonished look on my way out, if I did it was because that's exactly how I felt. Now I needed to hit the pool table while I sort out my thoughts. I couldn't believe that she'd attacked Rev, or even begin to understand what could have brought that on. But speaking of Rev, maybe he might be of some help. I called him on the walk over to the clubhouse.

"Hey, Rev."

"Hi, Murph." He sounded down.

"You alright?"

"No, not really. One of my parishioners was murdered last night; she was stabbed to death."

Suddenly I felt embarrassed about calling him just because I was in a spat with Lindsay. "Here? On ESVA?"

"Yes. Sweetest lady in the world, she wouldn't hurt a fly."

"Have they caught the guy?" I mentally kicked myself, automatically thinking that it must've been a man even without knowing any of the facts. Just as Lindsay had filed Rev in the "He's a guy" column, almost accusing him of using women. Yes, women do stab other women, though only a fraction as often as men stab women.

"No, and from what little the cops have told me, they don't have much in the way of clues or suspects. Heck, they don't even know what the motive was. Almost like it was a random attack. Just doesn't make any sense."

"Was she robbed or..." I didn't want to say it.

"No! No, she wasn't raped or molested in any way, and nothing was taken, not that she had much worth taking. Lived in an old modest house she inherited from her family. She was one of the ones that the church had helped out because she'd been struggling just to get by. And she had just started a new job. Remember that lady I told you about that used to work for the Mole before her conscience got to her? This was her."

"So, it happened at home?" I only asked because he sounded like he wanted to talk about it, to get it off his chest.

"Yes. No forced entry, so she let her killer into the house. That was about the only lead the cops do have, they are pretty sure she must've known her killer. Trusted her killer. And she died because of it. It's a crazy world we live in Murph. Evil finds its way into every corner."

"Yeah, Rev, and I'm sorry it found its way to your flock." I got a sudden mental image of a wolf and a flock of sheep. And I know Rev wants to be the protector of everyone in his church, but like the shepherd watching his sheep, he couldn't be everywhere, watching over every single person all of the time. But I knew this, minister or not, if Rev ever found the person who did this, there's a good chance he'd go back to his old waterman's ways for a few minutes. At least until the cops showed up to collect whatever was left of the murderer.

"Hey, thanks. But you didn't call to hear my problems. What's up?"

"I don't even remember," I lied. "But no doubt whatever it was can wait."

I WAS WELL into my second Chuck's Martini and my third practice game when the last voice I expected to hear tonight came from behind me.

"She's feeling kind of left behind."

I turned and faced Dawn. "Did Linds call you?"

"Yes, and I'd appreciate you not telling her I was here."

That caught me a little off guard, but I nodded and then asked, "What do you mean, left behind?"

"It's not her fault, Murph. It's not yours, either. I'm kind of to blame, though not really. Linds and Kari used to be so tight, then Kari got married and now they don't get to spend as much time together. She's worried that the same thing will happen to her and me, and I guess it already has a little bit. She had a lot of stuff planned for the two of us to do now that I'm back from my honeymoon, but I don't have the time I used to have, either."

That made some sense. I said, "She set Kari up with Marlin, and they lived together here before getting married. Nothing changed about that, other than Kari has gotten busier with work. And you and Case have been together for over two years, it's not like much is going to change with you guys either."

"I know. I'm not saying that it's completely true, I'm just telling you what she's feeling. Having that woman climb up and hug you today did not help the situation. And not to bring up a sore point, but our joint history isn't the most reassuring one for her."

Awkward. Very awkward. "And I'm sorry about that."

"I know you are, Murph. As Casey says, it's water past the stern. And we both ended up where we were always supposed to be, even if we couldn't see it at the time. Now you just need to make sure you can stay there."

Wow. That really shook me. I don't know what those two said to each other on the way back from *Bayside,* but I hope they weren't talking about this. Then again, I guess it was.

"Thanks, Dawn. That means a lot."

"Oh, don't misunderstand me here. I'm not doing this for you. At least not most of it. I'm doing this for Linds, because like I said, you guys are meant to be together. Okay, I may be doing a tiny bit of it for you, but the bigger part is for her."

"Then tell me what to do?"

"Don't leave me an opening like that." She smiled, then looked serious. "Be extra attentive and take her out more often, and not just here. Let her know she's not stuck in a rut. Make her feel more secure. And…" She hesitated a beat, "…you might want to discuss setting a wedding date."

"A wedding date?"

"Yes, Murph, a real, concrete wedding date. You know, the end game of an engagement? And I don't mean tomorrow, but a fixed point in time she can start planning for. The last thing you want right now is to go to dinner with that preacher's daughter and have her ask Linds, 'So, when is the big day?' and she doesn't have an answer to give her. That wouldn't exactly be like declaring an open season on you, since you two are engaged. But this goes back to that whole 'wanting to make her feel more secure' bit, especially around other single women. For some people, long engagements can signal insincerity."

"You and Casey were engaged for like two years."

"Again, I'm not trying to pick on you here, but your history and Casey's are nowhere near the same. I never for a second was insecure about our engagement. If you'll recall, it was Casey, not me, who pushed for that first wedding."

Several months ago, Casey and Dawn were first married aboard Lady Dawn, just offshore. That service had been just for close friends, and I was his best man. The big wedding up in Maryland was really for her parents and their friends. But she was right, it had been Casey that had gotten antsy and wanted the first one done here. I suddenly realized that I had been nodding as she talked. What she had said made sense, at least from a woman's perspective.

"Thanks, Dawn, I appreciate the advice."

"Yeah well, don't mention it. Especially to Lindsay. Remember, I was never here." She gave me a stern look.

"Got it. Forgot it already."

"The best thing you've said today."

· · ·

I WALKED into the salon of *OCT* where Lindsay was watching television and having a drink. She looked up at me, not an icy look, but not the friendliest one either.

"Hey," I said.

"Hey."

Yep, I'm still in trouble.

"Can we talk?"

She silently picked up the remote and turned the television off. Meaning that I was in really big trouble, the kind that demands full attention to the conversation. This was not going to be a "just mute the sound" kind of chat. She put the remote down and crossed her arms. Crap. This keeps getting worse. I sat down on the couch next to her, but she scooted over away from me, turning more sideways, toward me.

I said, "I've been thinking."

"Did you strain anything?"

Wow. Much worse than I thought. I ignored the jab and kept talking.

"When they get back with *Privacy*, I'll call Sandra and beg off for dinner."

"Like hell, you will. We accepted, and we're going."

"I thought you didn't like her and didn't want to go?"

"I don't, and I don't. But we're going."

Why is it that women and relationships can be more complicated than quantum physics? "Okaaay. Then let's at least have something to talk about when we go over there."

"What do you have in mind?"

"How about our wedding? Let's go ahead and set a date." I figured at this point she would get all happy and bubbly, but thaaat didn't happen.

"How about 'no.' I'm not going over there and talking about our wedding with a total stranger."

At this point, I got nothing. Total loss for words. That was my best shot, or so I thought. No point in opening my mouth, I'll only shove a foot in it, so I grabbed the remote and turned the television back on.

Then I got up and made my third vodka and took it with me into the shower.

I downed the drink, reached around the curtain, and set the empty glass on the countertop. Ten minutes later the curtain opened slightly, and Lindsay handed me a full glass.

"Did you mean it about setting a date?"

"Wouldn't have said it if I didn't," I replied.

She opened the curtain a little more.

"Think there's room for me in there too?"

I smiled. "Always has been, and that didn't change." I grabbed her arm, and pulled her in with me, fully clothed, and she shrieked.

"Not in my clothes!" Then her angry face faded into a grin.

"Right. We'll work on that part."

14

AMBUSHED

I took my first cup of coffee up onto our sundeck and uncovered one of the padded outdoor chairs. A thick layer of frost had formed on the covers overnight, the first of the season, and I could see my breath in the air. But that's part of the price you pay for a spectacularly clear ESVA fall morning. The sun seemed to be shining brighter than it had all summer. I watched as a pair of sea ducks flew past overhead. It was time for the changing of the guard as the waterfowl arrived for the winter and most of the pelicans and seagulls went south, seeking warmer climes.

"Spectacular morning!"

I looked past the Denton's *Why Knot,* berthed next to us, and spotted Marlin looking at me from the top deck of *Tied Knot,* their houseboat home that was berthed just beyond their vintage Chris Craft. Like me, he was wearing a thick jacket to ward off the cold morning air.

"Great minds think alike. I love having coffee outside in the fall," I said. He raised his mug in silent agreement.

"Hey, Murph, you guys want to have dinner with us tonight at the *Fin*? We haven't seen much of you two lately, and I'm about to get super busy with *Tuna Hunters* starting to film next week."

Darn! Why couldn't Marlin have asked yesterday? "Sure! Come on over here first at about 7:30 for drinks, then we'll walk over." The *Fin and Steak* is a higher-end restaurant here at *Mallard Cove*, with a great view right down the marina's inlet and to the open water beyond.

"Done! See you then. Got to go, my coffee's at low tide."

I waved, and he disappeared. Then a few minutes later a mane of blond hair cascaded over my shoulder as Lindsay gave me a one-armed hug from behind, her other hand holding a steaming coffee mug over to my side.

"Morning, Babe. Who were you talking to?"

"Marlin. They invited us out to the *Fin* tonight. Told them to meet us here at 7:30 for drinks. That okay?"

I got a long kiss for an answer, so I guess it is. Then she uncovered another chair and scooted it closer to me, smiling. What a difference twelve hours can make.

"What's on the agenda today, Babe?" She asked.

"Well, I thought instead of going out to a regular brunch, we'll go have 'Chinese breakfast' at that place you love over in VA Beach. Then we'll play it by ear. Maybe spend the day over there."

The smile got wider.

"I love dim sum!"

"I know."

How Lindsay keeps her great figure but can still do major damage on dim sum is one of life's great mysteries. If you've never had dim sum, you have yet to truly live. They bring a parade of carts around, piled high with all kinds of small dishes of Chinese delicacies. Everything from noodles to potstickers, all kinds of assorted dumplings, shrimp balls, and sticky rice wrapped in lotus leaves. Carbohydrate city, but somehow she doesn't ever gain an ounce.

"Think we could go to the mall afterward?"

"Sure."

"I'm going to go change."

I said, "You look fine like that."

She gave me a look like I was nuts. But in jeans, and a pastel tee shirt with one of my flannels as a coat, to me she looked great. I held up my now empty mug with a hopeful look as she passed by, but all I got in return was a scowl.

"I'm buying you dim sum and I have to get my own coffee?"

I was kidding, of course. Sort of. My plea fell on deaf ears as she disappeared down the stairs. I followed a minute later, making a "to go" cup, then went back outside to continue enjoying a fantastic morning. As I stepped on the dock Dawn was walking by with Bimini, taking a lap around the compound.

"Things are much better this morning. Thank you," I said.

"I already know. We've been texting back and forth. Dim sum was a good move."

"I'm a sucker for sticky rice. Hey, you guys want to come along?"

"Ordinarily yes, but you need to have a day out, just the two of you. So go and have fun."

THE MOLE WAS ALREADY HAVING breakfast with Sandra when Marty showed up at the table.

"Good morning. Better day today?" He asked his son.

"It's the Sabbath, this trip was a bad idea. I need to be at our church."

The Mole was again put off by his son's negative, complaining tone. "We will soon enough. But today we are going to continue relaxing and being pampered because we've deserved it."

"Deserved it? What have we done to *deserve* anything? And did you ever stop to think that by patronizing this place today, you are encouraging all these people to break the Sabbath by having to show up and serve you?" He scowled as he said it.

"People have the free will to choose their employment. I'm not forcing them to do anything. As far as what I've deserved, at least I've built something! All you've done son is suck at the teat of our church your whole life! Yet you dare to question what I deserve? It's been you that has acted as a self-entitled wannabe!" The Mole was getting worked up.

Sandra put a hand on her father's arm, distracting him and trying to get him to calm down.

"Father, remember your blood pressure. Marty, stop antagonizing him."

Marty looked at her and replied in a mocking tone, "Sandra, shut up!" He turned to the Mole, "I'll say what I want to when I want to. You both are supposed to think of others, serve others, to help make their lives better. But it's *you* that is acting entitled. *Both* of you!"

"Martin! Why don't you go pray for guidance, because you've lost your way." The Mole was now red-faced and struggling to maintain his composure.

"I'm the one that has found his way and am on the path of righteousness, father. You would be well served to take your own advice and pray for forgiveness!" He stormed out of the yacht and down the dock.

The Mole's brow furrowed. "He is getting more and more erratic, Sandra. When we get back, I'm going to have to relieve him of his duties at the church restoration and the outreach ministry. I hate to do this, but I'll need you to take all that over in addition to your normal responsibilities."

"I've already had to follow up behind him as it is, so it won't be that much different now. I agree with you, we can't risk having him making comments like he was this morning out in public. Especially not criticizing the prosperity gospel in favor of whatever his warped interpretation is called. But what do we do with him? How can we stop him from making statements in public?"

The Mole silently thought a minute before answering. "We send him on a missionary trip overseas. Maybe Haiti, or Africa. It gets him far enough away from here that if he starts spouting off, none of the U.S. media will be around to hear him. It also lends tax audit credibility to our church, just in case. We make him the head of our new missionary arm that we'll create around him."

Sandra nodded slowly as she thought. "It's perfect! We can also send a cameraman with him for the first part of it and use some handpicked clips in our ads. We'll ask for donations so we can do more to help impoverished people."

"I like it! Instead of hiding him, we spotlight his work for the church and show how sales of the prayer cube will help to finance our mission work. Give people yet another reason to buy one." The Mole interlaced his fingers and rubbed his thumbs together as he stared off into the distance, lost in thought as he considered all the angles. He refocused on his daughter. "It's perfect, let's get started on it first thing tomorrow."

THE CHINESE RESTAURANT used to be a grocery store, and they need every square inch of that huge space on Saturdays and Sundays, which is when they serve dim sum. It's always full on the weekends and usually has a fifteen-to-thirty-minute wait outside to get in. It's that busy, and that popular with the locals. So, after arriving mid-morning and finally finding a parking space a block away, we were patiently standing in line on the sidewalk in the overflowing parking lot. That's when something hit me in the back of my head that felt like a baseball bat. I went down to my hands and knees and was getting kicked in my ribcage before I could even regain my senses and stand back up.

Suddenly the attack ceased as quickly as it had begun, and I heard Lindsay cursing first, and then crying out in pain. I struggled back to my feet and saw that Branson had hold of Lindsay by her hair with his good hand. Keller was yanking on the other arm that had his plaster cast with both hands, trying desperately to pull him away from Linds. She stomped down hard on Branson's foot, and it was his turn to yell in pain. That's when he shoved her head into the concrete block wall, causing her knees to buckle.

This had given me just enough time to get back up on my feet. I grabbed his shirt and yanked him away from her then started wailing on his face with both fists. He let go of her hair to try and block my fists with that one good hand.

Even though Branson is taller and outweighs me, I have two things in my favor, I was in a blind rage, and Keller still hadn't let go of his cast. It took two big guys from the line to pull me off Branson after he finally went down hard on the concrete sidewalk. He ended up in a sitting position with his back against the same wall that he had bashed Lindsay's head against.

"Babe, stop! I'm okay."

Hearing Lindsay's voice helped pull me out of my rage, and I saw her standing up slowly. I shook both guys off of me and stepped over to help steady her. She was feeling the back of her head and winced when her hand reached the knot that had already started to swell.

Some guy in the crowd that had formed around us said, "I called the cops."

"What? No police, we aren't going to press any charges," Keller said.

"No, but I am! Assault and battery on both Lindsay and me," I replied.

"You do that, and we'll report you to the Coast Guard for trying to sink us this morning." While Branson wasn't in a hurry to stand up, he didn't mind running his mouth while sitting down.

"You know, we weren't going to get them involved, but since we have the whole thing on video showing you two ramming Martin Stoneman's boat multiple times, that's not a bad idea. It also shows how we were just coming to their aid, so yeah, let's call the 'Coasties,' too."

Somebody in the line asked, "Martin Stoneman, the preacher? These guys tried ramming his boat? Oh, and I got this whole thing on video, too. From the part where he was kickin' you on the ground. I didn't get the first part when he hit you over the head with his cast. But I'll be glad to tell that to the cops and show 'em my video."

"Thanks, man! Yeah, your video and ours might just be worth some money to one of those tabloid channels, since these jerks are the 'reverends' who bought Stoneman's old show." I wanted this out in the open, and for these guys to get what they deserved.

"I'll pay you for that video!" Keller's face had gone ashen.

The guy with the video said, "Reverends, huh? How come you two ain't in church right now? And since when does a 'reverend' sucker punch somebody with his cast? I bet one of those other shows will pay big bucks for it."

Keller replied, "I'll give you a thousand dollars cash not to talk to the cops or show them that video."

"I'll make it five grand," Branson said from down on the ground.

"Huh. If you'll pay five grand, one of those other shows will pay a lot more than that, especially when you go to jail!" He winked at me and said, "Don't worry man, I ain't gonna cave on you. I'll tell the cops everything."

We heard a siren in the distance, then thirty seconds later a police car pulled up next to the sidewalk. A minute later another cop car pulled up, followed by the paramedics. After taking statements, viewing the video, and forwarding a copy to the police station, the cops handcuffed Branson and had the medics check him out. Then they checked Lindsay and finally me. Both of us had very sore lumps on the backs of our heads, but otherwise, we were okay. Somehow both of us had escaped without a concussion. However, Branson was going to need a few stitches and a tooth capped. I had done quite a tap-dance on his face.

I don't know what made me happier, when they loaded him in the back of a squad car, or when it was finally our turn to get a table in the restaurant. I know my new friend with the video was happy after he asked for his check, but his server told him Lindsay and I had already picked up his tab. He was making out like a bandit today.

After we ate, neither of us felt like hitting the mall, since we both now had slight headaches. We agreed that a good form of medication would be a few beers in the $C2$ hot tub, so we headed for the Chesapeake Bay Bridge-Tunnel, or CBBT. It's a seventeen-mile trek from VA Beach to ESVA. The CBBT goes over and under the mouth of the bay and across Fisherman Island and ends right next to *Mallard Cove*. I was never so happy to drive through the gate to the little cove as I am right now. The cooler temperature had found its way into my ribs and muscle tissue that Branson had bruised, and I was starting to ache. That hot tub was just what the doctor ordered.

Linds packed a small cooler with ice so that we can keep a few spare beers close to the hot tub without having to get out. The hot water was soothing, and the beer was so relaxing; this was the best I'd felt since getting pounded.

"I hope you have more beer in that cooler."

I looked over to see Sandy coming up the walk. He was carrying a big but shallow cardboard box.

"The hundred-yard walk make you thirsty, you old geezer?" I needled him.

"Hell, everything makes me thirsty when it comes to your beer!" He came over to the cooler and helped himself.

"You know there's more over in the clubhouse, right?" I asked.

"Yeah, but from the looks of things you won't have to get out and refill it until after another round, so this'll do." Sandy took off his shirt and stepped into the tub. "Man, this feels good. I'm going to miss this."

Linds asked, "When are you headed to Florida?"

"Tomorrow. Going to dinner with Gilligan and his bride tonight. Figured I'd give Micah and Jeff a little time to themselves today since we're all loaded, fueled, and ready, then we'll leave out in the morning. We're starting via the Intracoastal route, stopping at Coinjock, North Carolina, tomorrow night, and then Ocracoke Island the next. One last trip down to the Keys."

Jeff is a member of Casey and Dawn's crew. He runs their sport fisherman, *Predator*, and doubles on *Lady Dawn* when needed. He and Micah have been an item for quite a while.

I nodded, having done that trip several times before. "Good stops. Wait, what do you mean, 'one last trip,' aren't you coming back?"

"Yeah, I'm coming back. I said one more trip *down*. But like you kids, I'm tired of running back and forth a thousand miles at a time. And Micah is getting tired of leaving Jeff in the winter. I'm going to bring the boat back up here next spring, and here it, and Micah will stay. I'll fly back and forth from now on. Gonna buy a condo down there like the rest of the world, then fly back and forth as I please without having to face that long trip in 'the ditch.' And if a hurricane wipes out the condo, oh well, that's what insurance is for."

Sandy is from the Keys, and that's where most of his family still resides. He still has a fishing outfitter store in Islamorada. After his wife died, he sold his house and moved aboard his fifty-five-foot trawler, deciding to travel with the seasons. His sisters were concerned about him traveling alone since he was in his mid-sixties at that point and the trawler was too much boat to try to handle by himself. Micah and her other cousin, Carol Davis, volunteered to work on the boat in exchange for room and board as well as help to launch their own writing careers. As a bestselling author, his guidance, as well as his recommendations, were huge boosts for them.

Carol fell in love with a young ESVA entrepreneur, Tyler MacKenzie, and the two operate a non-profit camp for people with disabilities that they started along with Eric Clarke. Carol became a full-time ESVA resident two years ago. Now it looks like Micah is headed toward becoming one as well.

Lindsay asked, "What about the store?"

"I'm setting up an 'earn out' purchase for the manager. She's been with my store for two decades, starting when she was just a teenager. And I don't want to have to worry about the place anymore. I'll make her a great deal, and it'll be a good living for her. Writing's my main income anyway."

Sandy took a long draw off his beer and I matched him, draining mine. Then I had to get partway out of the tub to reach the cooler which he had moved.

"Holy crap! What the hell happened to you?" Sandy asked. The bruises on my ribs were starting to show up, in a big way. Full-on Technicolor.

"Met up with your pal Branson again. But don't worry, he looks a lot worse than me, and he's a guest of the City of Virginia Beach right now."

"When are you going to learn that you two don't play well together?" Dawn asked as she came up the walk with Casey. Everybody had the same idea today since fall Sunday afternoons are perfect hot tub weather. Fortunately, she and Casey had built this one large enough to easily hold all of us.

Lindsay filled everyone in on what had happened to us in VA Beach. As she finished, Casey's phone rang. He had a short conversation, then looked up something on the internet and whistled.

"That was Rikki. ESVA Security has a program that watches out for all of our names as well as our properties, and you just went viral. The video of the two of you and Branson was just posted on the website of one of those television 'tell all' shows. You really downplayed what happened. Now the irreverent reverend is quite a hit online, and it'll probably be on their television show tomorrow night. And I'd say you were well on the way to getting even when they pulled you off of him."

Casey passed his phone around, with the video queued up.

"Watching Branson being loaded into a squad car almost made up for the rest of it. Plus, don't forget that it's Sunday, meaning he won't be arraigned until tomorrow morning at the very earliest. It's going to be a very long night for him." I grinned as I opened my new beer.

"Hey Casey, that box is for you. A little thanks for letting me dock here this year." Sandy pointed to the box he'd brought with him.

Casey pulled a custom teak sign out of the box. Under numerous coats of varnish were gold leaf letters spelling out *"Casey's Cove."*

"This is beautiful, Sandy, but you didn't need to do it. Thank you!"

"Yeah, well, you named the clubhouse, but you didn't name your mini-marina, so I named it for you."

"It's perfect, Sandy!" Dawn said.

Sandy replied, "I figured it would look good on the front of the boathouse, next to the door. It'll remind you kids of me until I get back next spring."

"That's exactly where I thought of putting it, too. Nice!"

Sandy beamed. Casey is the proverbial "man who has everything" that's so tough to shop for. But he'd hit it out of the park with this one. And I knew Sandy was right, we'll think of him all through this winter every time we see that sign.

A FEW HOURS LATER, Sandra was waiting at the side rail of *Privacy*, looking at her watch. They were now ten minutes late leaving *Bayside* because Marty had not yet boarded, and he wasn't answering his phone. They wanted to be out on the Chesapeake to have an unobstructed view of the sunset, and if he didn't get here soon, they would miss it. Finally, she spotted her brother coming down the dock, and she went down to intercept him.

"Where have you been? We're late!"

"Since when are you, my boss? And we shouldn't leave until after sundown, and the conclusion of the Sabbath. For your information, I have been praying all day for both your soul as well as our father's. That you both might see the error of your ways and repent. And that I might be forgiven for my sins as well. But most of all that you will stop leading our church down this false road of the prosperity gospel."

"Our church was built on the prosperity gospel, and we aren't about to change that. I hoped that you would find yourself through your prayer today. But if you don't get on the boat, you'll need to find a way home as well." She turned and started up the gangway, then looked up at the captain who was leaning over the rail on the flybridge. "Let's get underway."

Martin followed her up the gangway, but instead of continuing down the side deck and up the stairway to the flybridge, he went forward to the seating area in the bow to be by himself. His eyes had been opened further today to the wickedness of his family and their minions who willingly and even enthusiastically break God's laws. The church, Marty's church, must be protected at all costs, even from them. It was not too late if they wished to repent and turn their lives around, but that was not up to him. He was merely the instrument of vengeance and would become the true leader and reform the church. He had come to realize today that this is what he was born to do, it is his purpose for being here.

CINDY HAD BEEN on her way down the dock when Sandra confronted Marty. It was customary for someone in the resort staff to see large customers off when they departed. However, she stopped in her tracks when she overheard their conversation. She retreated, deciding a handwritten note in the mail would do fine instead.

15

MAN OVERBOARD

"*The Fin*," as everyone called the *Fin and Steak*, was an elegant dockside restaurant. Linen tablecloths and napkins, all the servers dressed in black pants and tuxedo shirts, the freshest seafood, and a wide selection of aged beef with a wine list to compliment every dish. Even though I own part of it, I don't come here that often. It's a little dressier than what I normally like, and the *Cove Restaurant* is more my style. Kari designed the entire layout of Mallard Cove, and she added the *Fin* as a higher level of dining for our customers that are used to that. It works, and Lindsay is loving the place tonight. I made a mental note to bring her here more often.

The truth is that I'd gotten so comfortable with Lindsay, we like so many of the same things, that I hadn't been giving enough consideration to the things that were more *her* favorites than *ours* or *mine*. Thanks to Dawn, that was something I was going to change.

Talking with him tonight, you would never know that Marlin was on the eve of a very hectic filming season. Two and a half months of non-stop filming of action as well as filler rolls followed by months of editing. Granted, he's the executive producer and wouldn't be doing all the physical work. But he and the other executive producer are responsible for making sure it all gets done, so no more days off for a while. The northern boats have already arrived, and Jimbo has brought the *Can Do* over from Deltaville.

But Marlin is as cool as a cucumber, despite having millions of dollars of foundation money already invested in the upcoming season. He was enjoying himself tonight, as was Kari. She and Lindsay were going on, non-stop, about wedding stuff. This is just getting started since the date we chose is eleven months away, close to Casey and Dawn's first anniversary. The one of their second wedding. I don't know which one of theirs counts, the first or the second.

"Murph? You here?" Marlin chuckled, having caught me lost in my thoughts.

"Hmmm? Uh, yeah, sorry."

Kari asked, "We were wondering if you had any ideas for your honeymoon location."

"Hadn't thought about it yet. Gimme a break, we only set the date last night."

"Don't worry, I'll let you know where we're going. I learned from Dawn, just tell him when to be there, and do all the planning yourself," Lindsay said, and the three of them laughed. I joined in since I knew it wasn't far from the truth. I quickly steered the conversation to ask about the other things the Denton's Fishing Foundation had been working on. Safer territory. Fortunately, we didn't revisit wedding plans right away.

We were seated next to one of the big windows that overlook the marina. The cooler fall weather had already created that crisp, ultra-clear air at night that makes lights on the water shimmer and sparkle. Not a lot of traffic tonight until I caught sight of *Privacy* out beyond the breakwater, making its turn for the basin inlet. It truly is a magnificent-looking vessel, and pretty to see at night. The others joined me in watching her maneuver as she pulled in and tied up.

Lindsay commented, "I hope the Mole appreciates how lucky he was to get the crew that came with that boat. If the previous owner had been moving to another yacht instead of getting out of boating altogether, he'd have had a hard time finding such great people with as much knowledge of Westports as them, especially the captain, Gary Stevens."

She had no sooner finished saying that when every light aboard the yacht came on. We could see two crew members frantically searching for something up around the bow.

"I wonder what's going on there?" I remarked.

"Somebody probably lost a piece of jewelry or something," Kari suggested.

We shrugged it off and went back to our meal. We were just finishing dessert when a Coast Guard M60 Jayhawk helicopter made a slow pass offshore, its forward-looking infrared (FLIR) pod scanning the water ahead. Then a rescue boat from Coast Guard Station Cape Charles came screaming around the corner of the jetty, its blue strobe flashing. They pulled into the marina, going straight over to *Privacy*. We lost sight of it behind the big hull.

"This isn't just over some lost jewelry," Marlin said.

"Yeah, no, it's not. But whatever it's about isn't good," I said.

"I'VE CHANGED MY MIND, I don't want to wait until tomorrow, I want to tell Martin about the changes tonight. I don't want to take a chance on someone outside the family hearing him criticizing our church again before we get the chance to talk," the Mole said. He and Sandra were sitting in the salon on Privacy as the captain made the turn into *Mallard Cove's* inlet. "I know how to frame this so that he's looking forward to the new position and getting excited about the new missionary arm of the church. Then he'll forget all about the griping and disagreements. Where is he?"

"He's up on the bow. I tried talking to him when we were abeam of Cape Charles, but his mood had worsened, so I left him alone up there."

Her father said, "Go tell him to come here, that I want to talk with him."

She nodded and left the room. She returned five minutes later, as they were pulling up alongside the dock.

"I can't find him anywhere! His phone is on the table next to his bed, and he hasn't packed yet."

The Mole directed, "Use the ship's intercom."

Sandra went to the nearest unit and called for him but got no answer. "All crew, has anyone seen Marty?" There was no response. "Captain Stevens, have you seen Marty?"

"The last time I saw him, the two of you were on the bow, Miss Stoneman."

"I can't find him anywhere! Please organize a search of the entire boat."

"Roger that." He switched to his headset radio, which all the crew was wearing for docking. "All crew, report to the bridge for assignments."

Ten minutes later the search had confirmed their worst fears, Marty wasn't onboard. Stevens radioed the Coast Guard with the toughest call he'd made in his career, an apparent "man overboard" in the dark water of the Chesapeake.

Within minutes two M60 Jayhawk helicopters took off from Coast Guard Air Station Elizabeth City in North Carolina. They covered the fifty-eight miles to ESVA in a little over twenty minutes, one of the two then continuing to Cape Charles, the last known position where Marty had been seen on the boat. That second helo would start a slower, methodical search from there, eventually meeting up with its twin.

Within an hour it was apparent to the pilots that there was no trace left of Marty on the surface of the bay. If he'd fallen in and drowned, it's likely his body would've slipped below the surface and stayed down. With the cooler fall temperature of the water, it might be days or even months before enough decomposition gasses formed in the remains to make them float.

Just to be certain, a forty-five-foot RB-M rescue boat and a twenty-nine-foot Small Crew rescue boat followed up behind the helos, using searchlights to scan the water and the shoreline, searching for any trace of Marty. But they came up as empty as the aircrews. He had simply vanished.

Both the Mole and his daughter as well as their crew had been told to stay in the salon while the crewmen from the rescue boat searched *Privacy*. One came up to the crewman in charge and whispered something in his ear, then the two left the salon together. They returned two minutes later, the lead one talking on the phone. He hung up and addressed everyone.

"I need you all to continue to stay in this room. This vessel is now a crime scene, and Virginia State Police crime lab techs are on their way."

"Did you find Marty?" Sandra urgently asked.

"No. But we found evidence of foul play, meaning that someone in this room knows exactly what happened to him."

Early the next morning, I went over to Sandy's trawler, *Epilogue*, to help him and Micah cast off. Jeff was already there on the dock, coiling their shore power cord and handing it up to her. I looked at Sandy up on his flybridge, waiting for his signal to uncleat the bow line. He signaled to Jeff to release the stern line, then turned to me and nodded. I tossed the line over the bow rail and watched as he started backing out of the slip.

Sandy grinned, and yelled from the bridge, "Hey, Murph, make sure you reload your 'fridge with Red Stripe before I get back!"

"I'll make sure to do that if you remember to bring back two things."

"What?"

"Some of that special Pilar rum, and stone crabs!"

He laughed. "Don't hold your breath!"

"Yeah, well, you either!"

Jeff and I watched as *Epilogue* slowly made its way out of the basin, with Micah waving to him as they disappeared out of sight.

"It's going to be a long winter," Jeff said.

"And how many roundtrip flights to the Keys have you already booked, lover boy?"

He grinned. "Four. Luckily, Casey and Dawn don't have any fishing or yacht trips planned until spring."

Lindsay joined me in walking over to the *Cove* for breakfast. Gary Stevens was coming up the dock as we approached. He looked like hell.

"Hey, Gary, we saw the Coasties board you last night, what happened?" I asked.

He shook his head. "Not exactly sure. But Marty went over the side somewhere between Cape Charles and here. State police crime scene guys think maybe someone attacked him, then dumped him overboard."

"What!" Lindsay exclaimed.

"Yeah. They found a bloody smear going from the top of the gunwale halfway down to the deck, some hairs stuck in the blood on the rail, and some blood drops on the deck. So, either he conked his head and was stunned, then stood back up and then fell over the rail, or he had help. The area was just out of sight from the flybridge, so I couldn't have seen what happened. But I'm not buying that he went over by himself, and neither are the cops. We've got those extra high safety rails that run from the bow back to the galley windows."

The Westport has a series of three-inch diameter stainless steel pipes about six feet long each that run horizontally, about ten inches above the gunwales. The ends are elbows that turn down toward the gunwales, firmly attaching them. These pipes block anyone from "bow riding" by sitting on top of the gunwales, a very dangerous stunt. Plenty of people have been killed or injured over the years by falling in front of boats this way.

Linds asked, "Who do they think might have done it?"

"I think they're looking at the daughter. I saw the two of them together up on the bow off Cape Charles just after the sun had set. It was still light enough to make out the two of them. They walked back out of view, and it was the last I saw of him."

The sightlines from the flybridge only allow the helmsman to see the first seven or eight feet of the bow. The curved seating area and table where Marty might have been sitting were completely out of his field of view because of the extended cabin roof. And since it was nightfall, there was only some dim deck lighting up on the bow, so as not to interfere with the captain's night vision, even though they did have a FLIR system.

"And that's not all, the son and the daughter kept getting into it the whole trip. I told the cops about it, and the boss got pissed off. He fired me as soon as they packed up and left, just a few minutes ago. The funny part is, the daughter just asked me back, but I've already been looking around. The boss isn't the greatest to work for, and life's too damn short, you know what I mean?"

I nodded. "Hey, sorry about all this. But right now, a job is a job. And if you do decide to leave and ever need somebody to give you a reference, have whoever it is call me."

"Thanks, but it's not your fault, Murph. I was happy to have the job until I got all the way hip-deep in it."

"But the daughter just overrode her old man? Sounds like she's either the real boss or soon will be. How's she to work with? She seemed pretty sharp when they were looking at boats and had a lot of input with him. I wouldn't jump ship without giving it a lot of thought, Gary."

He nodded. "Maybe you're right, I can always leave if I want after I get something else lined up. Now I'm going home to get some sleep, I've been up all night. Hope the Coasties find the son's body today."

We all knew that wasn't likely, but it would be nice for them to have some closure.

16

BLOOD FROM A STONE

"You should've made a deal with that guy for the damn video, Keller. I'd have never gone to jail. That was *your* fault."

Branson was furious after spending the night in jail and waiting in the courthouse holding cell for two hours to be arraigned, and another hour while Keller arranged for bail.

"Hey, it's not like you weren't trying to buy it too! He wouldn't sell. Apparently, he's a fan of Stoneman's. Drank some of that water he pedals and won big at the track or something, who knows. When he heard that we had rammed his boat, that was it. There was no amount of money that we could've given him for that footage."

Branson grunted in response, still angry. "Just get us back to the studio, I want to get to my office. There's going to be no getting that clip away from the cops, but maybe I can make the guy see reason."

"Uh, he already sold it."

"WHAT? To who?"

"To whom."

Branson looked at him like he was a complete idiot. "Whatever! Who'd he sell it to?"

"It was one of those video tabloids. They uploaded it to the internet yesterday, and they're putting it on television tonight."

"Well, that's just great," he said sarcastically. "Hopefully this won't cause too much damage."

Keller winced, and Branson noticed it.

"What?"

"The banker said he wants you to call whenever you... get out."

"He knows I was in jail?"

"Worse. He saw the video online."

Their one-year balloon note was almost up on the show. The bank had wanted to see their numbers after a year to figure out how much they would be willing to loan on it for the long run. The four members of Branson's group had invested most of their free cash, and they now needed to nail down long-term financing so they could get it all back out. They needed some of the recouped cash for the Gwynn's Island property. They had bought that and started renovating it with money from a line of credit, which was now almost tapped out.

Despite how cool it was outside and in the car, Branson's forehead had started sweating, and his palms were damp. He looked like he was about to be sick. He knew that taking on the Gwynn's Island property would put a squeeze on his cash, but he also knew there was good money to be made with it, and he had been counting on that if they were going to salvage the show.

BACK IN HIS office at the studio, Branson was on the phone with their banker.

"What do you mean you're calling the credit line? That cash is all tied up in our new property, and I have to have funds to continue operating. I still need to finish the renovations before we can get it open and then resell it!"

The banker replied, "It's tied to those South Carolina properties you put up as collateral which should just about cover it if you can't repay it now. And to let you know, you'll need to find permanent financing elsewhere for your television show and studio. We've seen the latest ratings, and with the financials you've shown us, we know you're right on the edge of needing a big cash infusion. Extending that note is not something we are willing to do for a show with sliding numbers."

"You bastard! You've made a ton of money off me for over twenty years! Now you're just going to bail on me?"

"Funny that you should mention bail, *reverend*. That's another thing, we prefer that our clients stay out of prison, and from the looks of that tape, it appears that you may have a tough time doing that.

"We'll be sending you the paperwork declining any loan extensions on the balloon note, and written notice calling the credit line. So, you'll need to start looking for permanent financing so you can avoid defaulting on the note, and then repay the line."

"Repay the line? With what!" Branson was now red in the face, "Listen to me you two-bit money whore, you're gonna give us an extension on all of it, and trust me, then I'll be out of your bank as fast as I can. So fast, it'll make your head spin! Hello? HELLO?"

The banker had hung up. Branson slammed the phone down in the cradle, almost breaking the receiver. If his good hand hadn't been in a cast, he probably could've broken it.

"KELLER! Get in here!" They used adjoining offices when he was in town. "KELLER!" He bellowed.

Keller opened the door between the two offices halfway.

"What?"

"Get in here!"

"I can hear you from here just fine."

There was no way he was going into Branson's office with him still in a rage. Branson was about to argue about it but decided to let it slide.

"Call the crew on Gwynn's Island and send 'em home."

Keller said, "But if we don't finish that project, we can't get it operating and spinning off cash."

"Yeah, Captain Obvious, you think I don't know that? The bank just called our line of credit which all our South Carolina properties are tied to. Plus they're refusing to re-fi the balloon on this place. So, call that realtor and dump the hotel. And while you're at it, dump that stupid water toy of yours."

Keller loved *Rev'd Up* almost as much as the Gwynn's Island project.

"We owe more on the boat than we can get for it."

"Then turn it back in to the dealership and let the finance company try to come after us. We've got to find a ton of cash, like yesterday, or we're gonna lose it all. They'll take all our Carolina properties if they foreclose! We'll have nothing left that's generating cash. If we can somehow repay that credit line, I might be able to stall them on the balloon note long enough to find somebody to lend us money on this place."

Keller withdrew back into his office and closed the door. He was panicking. When he'd found the deal on the show and studio, part of why he'd brought Branson in was his cash, and the other was his relationship with the bankers. Keller had never done a deal close to this size before, but he knew that Branson had, so the partners left it to him to handle the financing and purchase.

It wasn't until they had almost closed in the deal that they found out Branson was using mostly borrowed money in addition to theirs for the down payment, a fact he was hiding from the bank. His whole operation was a house of cards. The bankers would have never made the loan if they had known that. This meant the partners were all complicit in bank fraud since they all found this out before they signed. Branson made sure to tell the other three so they would all be in it together and have the same amount of risk. By that point, there was no backing out.

Keller knew that if this kept unraveling, not only would he be broke, but there was a good chance he'd be going to jail. And if it all did come down, he'd already decided he'd flip on Branson and the others if he could avoid jail time. Right now though he was going to do what he could to try and salvage this. Then he'd find some sucker to buy him out, and he'd get as far away from Branson as he could. The guy was a nightmare.

· · ·

"MISTER BRANSON, my name is Carter Dupree, and I represent Michael Murphy and Lindsay Davis."

Branson scowled at the speakerphone. "*Reverend* Branson."

"Yes, well, whatever. I'd say that ship has pretty much sailed."

"What do you want, Dupree?"

"It's not what I want, it's what you should want to do. And that's settle with my clients before we have to file suit and things get expensive."

"Settle with them? For *what!*"

"Um, assault and battery? That video will be great when it's played in front of a jury."

"And just what would your clients be looking for as a settlement?"

"Fifty thousand dollars. Each."

Branson laughed. "You go tell your clients to pound sand. If I had the hundred grand in cash, I damn sure wouldn't give it to them over a playground scuffle. So, go ahead and file your lawsuit. Only, if I were you, I wouldn't take it on contingency, counselor. You can't squeeze blood out of a stone, and I'd love nothing better than for that Murphy guy to be out of pocket for your legal fees."

For the second time this morning, Branson was hung up on by someone. The full realization of their situation was now dawning on him. He wasn't kidding, he'd have a hard time coming up with the hundred grand right now. Yet before he got involved in this damned television show, that much had been chump change. He could've drawn it out of his personal checking account. Everything in Virginia had been a disaster, the show, the studio, that hotel, all of it. There was one place he might be able to unload the television stuff, and he hated to do it, but it's what had to be done. If he got a contract in place, that should stall off the bank. He needed to make this deal face to face, he wasn't about to let anyone hang up on him. He picked up his car keys off the desk.

I HURRIED over to Kari's office. She'd had a message that Larry Donnelly, the realtor from Gwynn's Island, had called and wanted to talk about the hotel. On my way over Carter Dupree called me with a Branson update. After I hung up from Carter, I smiled. Truth was, I never expected Branson to pay, but out of spite, not for lack of funds. Giving me that information for free had been stupid on his part if Larry's call ended up being what I expected.

I walked into the office and saw Lindsay was already there with Kari. Bringing them up to speed, both of them started smiling, too. Kari picked up the phone and called Larry.

"Hi, Kari, thanks for returning my call. I have some good news! The hotel property is coming back on the market, and I wanted to give you the first shot at it before it gets listed."

"That's great, Larry. We might be interested in it, depending on the price, of course."

"They're only looking to get out of it what they have in it."

Kari laughed, and I wasn't sure if it was a forced laugh or not. She's a great negotiator.

"Well, seeing as how they overpaid for it in the first place, and we've seen the sub-par work that's been done which will now have to be redone, they're dreaming."

"Oh. Well, if you have a figure in mind, I'll be happy to take it back to them."

The figure that Kari quoted was two-thirds of their original purchase price. There was a long silence on the phone.

"Uh, I can almost guarantee they won't go for that. Their loan is much larger than that amount."

Kari said, "I don't know if you've seen the video that's online of one of the principals in the project committing battery on two of my partners. If not, you might want to watch it. Everything has a price, Larry. And if they want us to bail them out, anything over and above our offer is the price they'll pay for that. If they won't accept our price, we're very content to wait until it ends up in foreclosure, and we'll probably pick it up for even less from the bank. And they'll still be on the hook with their lender for the remainder. I'm being generous here."

"I'll see what I can do." He didn't sound optimistic.

"Have a nice day, Larry." She hung up.

Lindsay chuckled, "Have a nice day? Really?"

Kari replied, "Well, yeah. Think about it, he sold that with no other broker involved the first time. He got a full commission and didn't have to split it with anybody. Here he is again, trying to sell the same property twice in the same year, also without another broker involved. Anything he gets from it at this point is gravy. We're about to find out just how persuasive he can be."

"It's possible that he hit his head, got disoriented, fell or jumped over the side, and maybe he swam to shore but has amnesia. He's been so erratic lately." The Mole looked at Sandra, hoping to see some sign of agreement with his theory, but saw none.

"We have to start accepting that Marty may be gone, no matter how he ended up going over the side, father."

"I'll never believe that until they find... a body. Until then, he's just missing. Maybe he got picked up by a passing freighter or a crab boat or something." Stoneman was grasping at any straw he could find. He winced suddenly and put his hand on his stomach.

"What's wrong?" Sandra asked.

"I've got a stomachache. Probably the stress of what's happened. I'm going to go lay down in my stateroom."

Sandra's phone rang, and she grimaced when she saw who was calling.

"What? Who is it?"

"Branson."

"If you don't answer, he'll just keep calling back. You know how he is."

She sighed and answered the call. "Hello, reverend, this is a really bad time... un huh... I'm not there right now... what... okay, fine. I'll see you in fifteen minutes."

"What did he want?"

"To sell the show back to us."

Despite the circumstances, the Mole managed a wry smile. "Just as you predicted they would. Only it didn't take as long as we thought. They must have hit rock bottom already."

It had been their intent from the very start to unload the show, let somebody else take the hit as it dropped in value, then pick it back up at a fire sale.

"He's up at the compound, locked outside of the fence. While you get some rest, I'll go up and talk with him."

The Mole nodded and winced again as he got up. "You should get some rest as well, Sandra. Use the house while you're there and get some sleep."

He picked up his ever-present teacup and headed for his stateroom.

SANDRA USED the time alone during the drive to think over everything from last night in her mind. As erratic as Marty had been, she wouldn't have put it past him to have tried hurting himself. Maybe he started cutting himself and then couldn't continue because it hurt too much. Then he might've jumped and drowned himself, or maybe he swam to shore. Nothing was out of the realm of possibility with him the way he is now. She sincerely doubted that any of the crew would have been involved in him disappearing, they hardly knew him.

As she turned into the studio's driveway, she saw Branson's Cadillac up by the gate in the middle of the lane. She hit the remote opener and watched as it opened slightly, and then stopped. Sandra got out of her car to check the gate mechanism. As she walked toward the fence, she saw that Branson's driver's side window was open. Branson was inside, but he wasn't moving. In fact, he'd never move on his own again. His throat had been slashed and he was covered in blood.

17

DROPPING LIKE FLIES

After an hour of questioning about her relationship with Branson, her brother, and the other recent knife murder that happened to be an ex-employee, the Northampton County Sheriff begrudgingly let Sandra leave. He didn't like how the two murders and the disappearance all had close linkage to Sandra, but he had no evidence that she was directly connected to any of them. Her cell phone had been located at Mallard Cove when she received Branson's call, and she had dialed 911 immediately after arriving at the compound.

Even being that close to the house, Sandra wouldn't have had time to get cleaned up before the first deputy arrived on the scene. And whoever murdered Branson would've had to have a large amount of blood spattered on them. The sheriff let her know that she might be off the hook for now, but they would probably be questioning her again as their investigation continued.

Sandra drove back to *Mallard Cove* from the Sheriff's Office. She wanted to be the one to tell her father about Branson. He wasn't in the salon, so she went to his stateroom to see if he was awake. He was on top of the bedcovers, and he wasn't moving. But there was a pool of vomit next to his head.

"Father!" She rushed to his side and saw that while he was still breathing, his breaths were shallow. She picked up his wrist and found a very weak and slow pulse. Despite shaking him and patting his face, she couldn't get any kind of response.

I WATCHED through the windows at the brokerage as the first deputy's car came speeding into the parking lot, followed closely by a rescue squad van. The deputy and two paramedics raced down the dock to *Privacy*, where they disappeared onboard. Two other sheriff's cars pulled in, and those officers also hurried aboard. A few minutes later the paramedics reappeared, carrying the Mole on a backboard that they placed on a waiting wheeled gurney. Stoneman was very pale and didn't look good at all. They raced the gurney down the dock and to their van, loaded it aboard then took off with their lights on and siren screaming.

I turned my attention back to *Privacy*, where I didn't see any of the crew. A while later the sheriff himself arrived, followed by a couple of state police crime scene techs, their hands loaded with gear. Casey had been walking by when he noticed the commotion and stopped at the head of the dock to watch. I went out and joined him.

"What's up on *Privacy*?"

I shook my head. "Dunno. But a while ago they took the Mole out of here on a stretcher, and he didn't look good."

"Heart attack?"

"I don't know. They weren't doing CPR or anything, but he was white as a sheet. The sheriff and the crime lab techs wouldn't show up here for just a medical emergency."

A deputy emerged from the boat with Sandra behind him, followed by the sheriff. They loaded her in the back of the deputy's cruiser, and he sped off, followed closely by the sheriff in his car.

Casey said, "That doesn't look like Sandra's going to the hospital to check on her father."

"It didn't look like she was under arrest, since she wasn't in handcuffs. On the other hand, it didn't appear that she was free to go anywhere, either."

Another deputy's car pulled in behind us.

Casey commented, "Looks like we've had the entire motor pool from the sheriff's office here today."

I recognized the deputy that got out of the car, a guy named Canfield. He eats at the *Cove* regularly. To my surprise, he headed straight for me.

"Mister Murphy, I'd like to ask you about a few things if you don't mind."

"Of course not, deputy. What can I do for you?"

"Where have you been for the last three hours?"

Whoa, what the hell was this? "Why do you want to know that?"

"Reverend Thomas Branson was murdered this morning."

That hit me between the eyes, almost as much as being questioned, apparently in connection with it.

"And *I'm* a suspect?" I asked incredulously. Okay, it was more of a statement than a question.

"These are just some routine questions that we're asking of everyone who had contact with him recently. It's common knowledge that you two didn't like each other and that you might have been looking for some payback after that fight at the Chinese restaurant."

"Which is exactly why I sicced my lawyer on him this morning. We are, well, *were* about to file a lawsuit against him for battery, both me and my fiancée. I didn't want to kill him, just lighten his wallet a bit. And it's tough to get money out of a corpse."

He nodded. "So would you still mind telling me where you were?"

"Not at all, um, I was right here, in a meeting with our sales team since nine a.m." I motioned toward the brokerage office.

He looked a bit relieved, and a lot more friendly. "I'm assuming that they can verify that."

"Ask anyone in there."

"I will, thanks. And what about Miss Davis, do you know where she was and where I might find her?"

Casey spoke up, "She was on board our boat with my wife and me all morning. I'll be happy to take you over there to talk to them."

"I'd appreciate that, thanks."

I asked, "How was he murdered?"

"Knife attack up outside of the Stoneman's compound. Stabbed and had his throat cut."

"So, that's why Stoneman had his heart attack," I said.

He looked at me funny. "What makes you think Reverend Stoneman had a heart attack?"

"Well, they took him out on a gurney, he looked like crap, and now hearing that Branson died up at his place right after his kid disappears overboard, he is probably stressed out to the max. I know he has high blood pressure. Always drinking his special tea for it."

The deputy closed the little notebook that he had been writing in.

"Well, he's not stressed out or worried about his blood pressure anymore. He died at the hospital."

That was another shocker. I knew he didn't look good, but I hadn't expected him to die.

"Wait, why did you ask why I thought it was a heart attack? Does that have anything to do with all the crime scene techs that are onboard? I just figured it might be something to do with the son."

"I'm sorry, I can't comment on that." He turned to Casey, "Would you mind taking me to see Miss Davis after I confirm Mr. Murphy's whereabouts with his associates? I just need to verify everything with her and your wife."

By the look on his assistant's face in his doorway, he knew something was terribly wrong. So, what else was new today?

"Mr. Keller, there's a sheriff's detective out here…"

The detective shoved her aside as he pushed his way into the office. Keller was surprised since VA Beach wasn't part of a county. The sheriff's office ran the jail, and the security at the courthouse, and served legal papers. No way the bank could've acted this quickly, and as far as he knew, the sheriff's office didn't even have a detective. Then he saw by his identification the man was a Northampton sheriff's detective.

"Reverend Keller, I'm Detective Neeley of the Northampton Sheriff's Department. I hate to have to tell you this, but Reverend Branson is dead." The detective had pushed his way in specifically so that he could watch Keller's reaction to the news. And there was no faking his look of total shock. But he noted that there was also a complete lack of sorrow. As soon as Keller digested the news, the detective could see he was now lost in thought, and he took his time before asking the expected questions.

"How did this happen?"

"He was murdered in his car up in ESVA."

"It must've been Murphy!"

"Mr. Murphy was nowhere near the scene at the time of the murder, and neither was his fiancée, who I understand also had a grudge against him."

"They're suing him. Correction, they *were* suing him. He talked to their lawyer this morning."

The detective nodded. "We already know about that. But it's also a reason they wouldn't want Reverend Branson dead. Can you think of anyone else who might have wanted to hurt the reverend?"

"Thomas isn't... wasn't... the easiest person to get along with."

"Yet you were in partners with him in your ministry."

"Church," Keller corrected, almost distractedly. "In this church only. I'm involved with several ministries in South Carolina."

Keller was already pondering his next move since Branson had been the point man with the bankers. He was trying to decide if his death might somehow be used as a lever to extend their notes while things get reorganized or sold. But he was also worried that it might hasten any foreclosure action.

He continued, "And sometimes even in churches there are people who might not be the most pleasant to be around, detective. Yet they have a God-given talent that the church needs."

"What was Reverend Branson's?"

"His was a gift for handling financial matters. It's easy to forget that there's more than just a spiritual side to a church. Especially one that has a television ministry like ours. There is a business side behind it all, even though the ultimate goal of this particular 'business' is different from those you'll find listed on Wall Street. But we still need to take in more money than we spend. Thomas was in charge of making sure that we do."

"I need to search his office and see if there might be anything there that would point to anyone who he might have had issues with."

Keller nodded toward the door leading to the adjoining office. "Thomas used that office when he was here, which wasn't that often. His main office was back home in South Carolina, so I'm afraid you won't find much here."

"When you say not often, can you be more specific?"

"About once per quarter. That's when we have our board meetings. Thomas had very little contact with the members of this ministry other than then."

He led the detective into the other office which had no personal touches, and only a few file folders on top of the desk.

The detective remarked, "You're right, there's not a lot here."

"Yes, like I said, this wasn't his main office, and he had very little contact with the people here."

"Well, reverend, he had close contact with someone, enough to tick them off and want to kill him, using a knife. The ferocity of the attack indicated it was something personal, probably done by someone he knew."

Keller grimaced, for whatever reason he'd just assumed Branson had been shot. As big and mean as he was, he figured the killer wouldn't have wanted to get that close to the man. Suddenly he felt sick.

"Detective, if you need anything else, I'll be next door."

"There is one more thing, reverend, where were you this morning?"

"I was here, in my office. You can ask my assistant; I never left my desk."

18

TAKE THE DEAL

"This is crazy! People disappearing and now dead? I mean, Branson deserved a good butt-kicking, but not killing," Lindsay said.

I replied, "Tell that to my ribs." Casey and I had stayed behind with Dawn and Lindsay aboard *Lady Dawn* when Canfield left.

"It's too weird. Branson gets stabbed, Stoneman Junior drowns, and we don't know what happened to the Mole other than he wasn't stabbed, he didn't drown, and he didn't have a heart attack," Dawn commented.

I replied, "Yeah, but that friend of Rev's, their former employee, was stabbed, too. May have just been a coincidence that all these people had a connection and that it was the Stonemans. I'm thinking conspiracy of some sort."

"But what do they have to gain? And who would 'they' be?" Dawn asked.

"I don't know, but if I were that fellow Keller, I'd be nervous right now," Casey said. As soon as he finished saying that his phone rang. He went up to the galley so he wouldn't be interrupting our conversation in the salon. He returned a few minutes later.

"That was Rikki. She has a new protection client, Sandra Stoneman. Apparently, Keller isn't the only nervous one."

"Who could blame her? First, her brother disappears, then Branson dies, and now her father mysteriously dies." Dawn sounded sympathetic.

Casey shook his head. "Not so mysteriously. Cops told her that the Mole was poisoned. And, Branson was ambushed at the family compound, but they aren't convinced that he was the original target. The gate had been sabotaged; it only opened partway before it jammed. Only, Branson didn't know the code for the keypad or have a remote. He called Sandra when he couldn't get in, and she went straight up there from here, finding him already dead. She hadn't known he was going up there until he called.

"The sheriff's department thinks she might have been the original target. Let's say you were coming in here to the cove in your car, you hit your remote, the gate only opens a few feet and stops. The first thing you'd do is get out and check it or use the emergency release then slide the gate open manually. The perfect scenario for someone who wants to ambush you. This means the attacker was lying in wait and could've just walked away when Branson showed up instead of Sandra, but they didn't. To take that risk the attacker had to know and have something against Branson personally too.

"But whoever the culprit is got away clean. If Sandra was the original target, the killer is still out there, and probably hasn't given up on going after her. And since the same method was used, it's possible that Rev's parishioner was also killed by the same attacker, but why? This has got to have something to do with the Stonemans."

I asked, "So what are the reasons that people kill other people? Money, power, greed, love, jealousy, protection, property, what else?"

"With the Mole, I think you can dismiss love and jealousy. He wasn't that lovable, and I haven't seen any women hanging around, not even on their yacht trip," Lindsay said.

Dawn had been quietly leaning back in her seat, staring off into space. I knew that look. I asked, "What?"

She now refocused on me. "Maybe we're looking at the wrong common denominator. Maybe it's not Stoneman, but his church."

I found myself nodding at the idea. "Rev said his friend used to work for them, which means she had to have been a member of Mole's church because all their employees are required to be. He said she left because her conscience was bothering her, so that might automatically make her an enemy of the church. Keller and Branson were strongly against the Mole's new line of work, selling the prayer cubes and fundraising with the water pouches, the new church's source of income."

"Cindy told Rik that Marty and Sandra were at each other's throats over the spiritual direction of their church, having a big, loud argument about it on the dock at *Bayside*, right before they left," Casey said.

"Whoever is behind this is trying to protect the church," Dawn mused.

Casey said, "That or take it completely over. I've read where some of these mega-churches 'own' a string of other churches, all falling in lockstep behind it. Like when the Mole tried taking over Rev's church, or when that one church tried taking over that big religious theme park several years ago."

I asked, "Whatever happened with that, anyway?"

"Bankruptcy, then the land was all split up and developed except for the main church, which is still a church, now owned by another church. And most of the land was developed by other church organizations." Casey shook his head slightly.

"The Keller's and Branson's of the world," Lindsay said.

"Exactly," Casey replied.

I said, "Rev told me that everything was in the name of the church or its ministries, and I know the Mole put the title to the Westport into a separate ministry. Probably the same kind of one those other televangelists use for their private jets. Rev also said the Smithfield estate is owned by the church, as its parsonage."

"So, it's like having a private trust that doesn't pay taxes. The leaders get the use of it throughout their lifetimes, and then it gets passed to the new leaders coming up inside the church. If they're family members, it can go from generation to generation with no estate or inheritance taxes," Dawn was grasping the full concept.

Casey added, "Right, nothing to encumber the assets. We all think that we own our properties and projects, right? Try not paying the real estate taxes for two years and see what happens. Haven't done any estate planning? Your heirs better have a pile of cash if they want to keep it all when you die. But church properties can even sit idle without having to lay out a cent, so long as the church itself is still viable. And who's to say whether it is or isn't, since they don't have to report income and expenses.

"Now that the Mole and his son are dead, nothing changes. The yacht, the estate, and all the assets the church and its ministries own all stay the same. I'm assuming the only difference will be that Sandra Stoneman will get complete control of it now."

I argued, "But I got to see Sandra and the Mole interact. He was pretty accepting of her suggestions and let her take the lead on almost everything she wanted. She seemed to adore him, and she handled the yacht deal, dealt with the crew, the works. Why kill her old man who was already getting up there in age? Chances are he wouldn't have been around that much longer. Since the church owned everything, it wasn't like she was going to gain any assets that she didn't already have total access to. I mean, her father was already older, had high blood pressure, and refused to take anything for it. Just drank tea with that incredibly expensive honey to try and control it. The guy was a walking medical time bomb.

"Now the brother, on the other hand, was a problem for her. And she was admittedly the last one to see him alive. Getting rid of him could eliminate a huge thorn in her side."

Casey shared the rest of the conversation that Cindy had overheard between Marty and Sandra right before they left *Bayside*.

"So, he wanted to radically reform their church. Probably no more yacht, or spa weekends, and who knows what else if he got his way. Hey, those *Bayside* spa days are almost worth killing for," Lindsay said, mostly in jest.

I filed that one away for the next time I'm in the doghouse. "So, I get the part about wanting Marty out of the way, but again, why kill her father," I asked. Nobody had a quick answer for that one.

Then Dawn suggested, "Maybe we're still looking at this wrong. I agree that the church is the common denominator, but there are two camps in and around it. The ones who are for the 'prosperity gospel,' and those 'originalists' who read the Scriptures differently. The only two that we know of who were opposed to the prosperity interpretation are no longer around. Though two others who were strong proponents of it are also gone. Who did they tick off?"

I said, "Keller. He stands to benefit the most of all of them. He wanted the Mole to stop his cube and water businesses or ministries, whatever you want to call them. With him off the air, it cuts out what Keller sees as competition. Plus, I saw them quarreling on the dock that day. Then, we all saw him fighting with Branson aboard *Rev'd Up*. With him out of the picture, it makes his position in their 'television church' that much stronger. He'll be the leader."

Lindsay asked, "But why would Keller care at all about Stoneman's ex-employee? Why would he even know her?"

A funny look came over Casey's face. "He wouldn't because he didn't. We've been thinking there was only one killer. What if there were two? Sandra takes out Marty and their former employee to silence both of them. Then Keller takes out the Mole and Branson. They just happened to have the same solution for different problems, totally independent of each other. Then both of them end up running their respective churches without any interference. Problems solved."

I looked at both women and saw on their faces some of the same misgivings I was feeling. Was what Casey suggested possible? Yes. But as to whether it was probable, I was having a problem with that. I needed some air.

"Lunch at the *Cove*, my buy. It'll give us all some time to think on our walk over," I said.

. . .

WE GRABBED A BIG TABLE INSIDE, close to the wall. We no sooner had sat down than I spotted Rev coming in, and I waved him over. He took one of the two empty chairs.

"Crazy happenings lately," he remarked.

"We've been trying to figure it out all morning, and we might have done it," I told him our latest theory.

"I know you have at least part of it wrong. They just arrested my friend's younger cousin. The boy's a total meth-head, his brain is destroyed. He had gone to her house believing she had millions of dollars stashed away and killed her in a rage after he found out she didn't. He was still wearing his same bloody clothes when they caught up to him this morning."

"Which makes the rest of our theory that much stronger. Your friend's death bothered me as to how well it fits in," I said.

He nodded. "What bothers me is that if you're right, two other murderers are running around loose on ESVA."

Lindsay replied, "And one of them has a boat here in our marina. But we can't ask her to leave since she hasn't been arrested, much less convicted of anything. Casey can tell you there's a big difference between the two."

"Yes, I can. It sucks when your life gets turned upside down over something you didn't do. And they had more 'evidence' that pointed at me than there is that points at Sandra Stoneman. Right now, the only thing we have is conjecture and theory. I for one am not about to condemn someone solely on that."

I said, "I agree with both of you. Innocent until proven guilty. But it doesn't hurt to keep our eyes and ears open, especially if she's still a target and her attacker might follow her here. Until someone is charged and jailed, it would be a good idea for all of us to carry our handguns with us. You never know what might happen."

KELLER WAS LEANING BACK in his desk chair with his eyes closed. He knew it was over, that everything was crumbling around him. His only exposure in the television financing was the cash that he had put up in the beginning, and fortunately, Branson had put up the majority of it. Which was why he had brought him in on it in the first place. Keller hadn't even personally guaranteed the note.

He knew the cash was gone, and he could live with that if he could somehow manage to keep his two income-generating properties in South Carolina that were tied to the line of credit. Freeing those up would give him back the same income stream he had before he got involved in this mess.

That damned Murphy and his partners had made a ridiculously low offer on the Gwynn's Island property, and he had immediately dismissed it. But now he was thinking that if they had the cash and could close quickly, that amount plus the properties Branson had put up would be enough to repay the line.

Keller knew where he could borrow enough cash to buy the best pair of Branson's properties when the bank forecloses on them. While the interest rate wouldn't be as good as what Branson could have found, by putting a deal together the bank should jump on it and agree to drop any claim to his properties. They won't be stuck with real estate on their books while waiting for it to sell, something bank regulators hate seeing. Instead, they'll quickly recoup all the cash on the line of credit.

Keller would have to walk away from the show and studio, minus the cash he put up. But going back to Carolina with his properties plus the two of Branson's would give him double the income he used to have. Plus, he'd be back home, and the hell and gone away from Virginia. And he was never coming back.

HALFWAY BACK TO *Casey's Cove*, his phone rang. "Hey, Kari... what... you're kidding me! Heck yes, you told him we'll take it, right... yeah, we can do that. Thanks."

Dawn asked, "Take what?"

He broke out in an ear-to-ear grin. "The Gwynn's Island deal. At our price. Keller is bailing out of everything; the only stipulation is we have to close fast."

That's another thing I've learned from Casey, never be afraid to insult somebody with a lowball offer. You never know just how desperate they may be, and in Keller's case, I didn't feel one bit of remorse for taking advantage of that situation.

19

BAD TEA

The following day Sandra woke up on *Privacy,* after having slept through the night courtesy of a couple of sleeping pills. She hadn't slept at all the night before when Marty went overboard, and then losing her father on top of that yesterday morning was just too much. She had needed the release that came from the deep, drug-induced sleep.

But now the nightmare was back, and she had responsibilities that needed to be attended to. On her way up to the galley for breakfast, she found one of Rikki's associates sitting outside of her stateroom door. He accompanied her upstairs, then after breakfast insisted on driving her in his black Escalade to her appointment at the funeral home. She had an appointment with the funeral director to arrange her father's service.

On the way over she called the Coast Guard and found out that there was nothing new to report about Marty. As she hung up, she wondered if they would ever recover his body so that she could also arrange for his service as well. When they reached the funeral home, she insisted on going in alone and leaving her escort in the car. This was a personal mission, and she wanted privacy.

Almost an hour later, the Escalade was waiting for her at the covered entrance with her door already open. As she climbed in and sat down, she never felt the two stainless steel probes enter her chest before she was hit with 50,000 volts that raced through their connecting wires. Every inch of her body was in agony, and she couldn't move. She saw a rag moving toward her face and then smelled something sickeningly sweet as the world got fuzzy and black.

THIS MORNING LINDSAY and I had been late getting out of bed for reasons that were... uh... very much worth it. She went back to sleep soon after I got up. Rather than have the aroma from cooking bacon tease her back to consciousness, I decided to let the breakfast professionals at the *Cove* cook for me, giving her a chance to sleep in. A quick text to Casey confirmed that he was up for a walk over there with me and some conversation.

Casey met me on the dock, and I handed him a short "to-go" coffee that matched the one in my other hand. Steam from both cups was dissipating as fast as it left the liquid's surface in the face of a stiff and cold western breeze. At least today I had checked the weather app on my phone when I got up, and I was dressed for it. See, even us older dogs can learn a trick or two.

As we made our way to the restaurant I said, "I'm thinking of buying a boat."

"You already have two, Murph."

"Yeah, one that doesn't have any motors, and the other that uses ten gallons of fuel just sitting at the dock as it warms up."

"Then what kind of boat are we talking about?"

I replied, "An outboard that I can handle by myself."

"You've already got that with *Incognito*," he said.

"And you know how much I appreciate you letting me borrow her from time to time. But now that we are buying that Gwynn's Island property, I figure we'll be running over there more often. Thirty miles across the bay beats that hundred miles around it and rush hour traffic any day. But I don't want to have already 'gleeped' your boat on a day that you suddenly decide to go fishing."

Casey nodded, seeing the logic in my thinking. "Have any boats in mind?"

"Carlton Albury has an older thirty-one-foot Contender that's an insurance job. It was stolen, and the motors were removed. But he's got a used pair of Yamaha 250 horsepower outboards with low hours that he knows the history of. I can put the whole thing together cheaper than I could buy a new single-engine seventeen-foot Mako."

He looked like he approved. "Thirty-one feet should handle almost any day on the bay."

"Exactly."

"Have you run it past Lindsay yet?"

"Never have had to before."

"You weren't engaged with a wedding date set before. The old 'yours' and 'mine' thinking became 'ours' at that point, pal."

I stopped walking, thinking that over. Casey stopped and looked at me, obviously amused. "Just how far did you think this engagement through?"

I shot him a dirty look. "Far enough. I just have to get used to these kinds of things. But she'll love the idea."

"Pretty sure of yourself."

I nodded. "I know her. Plus, I'm going to name it *LNZ II* and she's sure to love that."

"Now you might be onto something."

We grabbed a two-top table and I ordered breakfast while Casey had another coffee, having already eaten earlier. He's a very early riser. Then in walked Deputy Canfield, who took the table next to us.

"Good morning, deputy," I said.

"Good morning, Mr. Murphy, Mr. Shaw."

"Casey."

"And Murph."

"Then call me Chuck."

I said, "Then I take it I'm off the suspect list for slicing and dicing Branson, and poisoning the Mole?"

He looked startled, then suspicious. "How did you know that Reverend Stoneman was poisoned?"

"Friends with friends in your office," I replied.

He relaxed again. "Oh. Sorry, that just isn't too well known. But I guess it doesn't matter, since you didn't have access to the yacht's pantry."

"Not after he bought it, though I showed him through it when he was in the market. So, he got poisoned onboard?"

"Yeah, oleander leaves, ground up into dust, and put in his tea."

I said, "Oleander leaves? Where would you get any of those around here? Those things grew like weeds back where we're from in Florida, but they don't like the cold. They don't go as far as North Carolina." Then it hit me. "And Branson was from South Carolina. He and Keller came aboard the last time I was on it."

Canfield nodded but didn't comment.

Casey looked thoughtful. "You know, both Junior and Senior Stoneman's made several charter trips to South Carolina on our jet when they were in the process of selling their tv show. And Junior made a one-day roundtrip down there on our prop plane last month. I figured he was just trying to save money since he was the only passenger and the prop plane charters for a fraction of the cost. But the jet trips were all charged to their ministry, and this last time my pilot said he paid in cash. That's why I remembered it since we get almost no cash business."

Canfield had his notebook out and was furiously jotting down what Casey said. He asked about the date and time of the flight, then handed Casey his card in case he found out anything more from his pilot. Then he got up and left without ordering.

I said, "Looks like you may have added another potential suspect to the mix."

"Especially since he was getting into it more and more with his sister and father. Though with his increasingly erratic behavior, I wonder if someone could have been poisoning him, too."

"Well, whoever got to his dad, they were all close enough to know about his tea habit. I wonder if they spiked the tea at his home too, or just the boat," I mused.

Casey said, "Sounds like it was only the boat, from what Canfield let on. I knew the stuff was poisonous but think about how much of it we added in the landscaping on the Florida properties over the years. I never gave it a second thought until now. I don't think there's a single gated community down there that doesn't have some in their plantings. The flowers are so bright, and they fill in nicely."

Our server brought my breakfast and warmed up both our coffees. Between bites, I asked, "You want to go look at the Contender with me?"

Casey set his mug down. "No way, not until after you take Lindsay over there first."

"Chicken," I ribbed him.

"No, I'm saving your butt. We're going to make a stop at the office on our way back, I'm going to help you. Plus, a little advice. A breakfast biscuit and an order of bacon to go."

"The biscuit already has bacon on it," I said.

"True, but the biscuit is for Lindsay. The bacon is for me, it's the price for my advice."

"Thanks, Babe!"

I had the re-warmed biscuit sandwich and a coffee waiting on the galley countertop for Lindsay as she emerged from our stateroom. I sat down in a bar chair next to her. "There's a method to my madness."

"Hmmph?"

Yeah, trying to talk through one of the *Cove's* oversized house-made biscuit sandwiches wasn't remotely possible. As she continued to eat, I laid out my case for needing an outboard boat of our own. From the slight nods I was getting, I was encouraged. Then I rolled out a three-foot stock picture of a thirty-one Contender with *LNZ II* superimposed on the side.

"Casey and Kari helped me with the picture part."

She set her sandwich down. "You've never had to ask me about boats before."

"True. But you were always there before, giving me advice on each one that I bought, sold, or traded. And we were never engaged before. You know the whole 'yours' and 'mine' is now 'ours' kind of thing."

She laughed. "Casey helped you with that, didn't he?"

"I'm hurt. Shocked, too. You don't think I could've realized that on my own?"

"No! Babe, I know you, and sorry, but you aren't tuned in to things like that. Since you had breakfast with him, I figure he gave you some advice."

It's scary how much she does know me. "Well, I guess you think he came up with the name, too."

"Don't get grumpy, and no, I think that part was all you. I'm flattered, by the way. So, when do we go see it?"

"Depends."

"On?"

"Whether you finish that sandwich here or in my truck on the way over."

THERE ARE SO many things that make Lindsay and I go well together, not the least of which is her ability to look at projects that others might turn their nose up at, but she can see the finished product in her mind. The Contender was one of these. It had been stolen last year, stripped, and dumped in the woods where it filled with leaves, the tannic acid staining the deck. The insurance company had already paid out on the loss and now wanted to recoup whatever they could get. My kind of deal.

"Let's get it. We'll make money on the deal just cleaning it up, Babe!"

That's why I want to marry this woman. We made an offer through Carlton, and by noon we owned it as well as the pair of used outboards. Then it was back to the *Cove* for a celebratory lunch and a quick change into working clothes that we wouldn't mind ruining if they got spattered with bleach. We were going to need gallons of the stuff.

We sat at the bar so that we could get in and out of there quickly. Andy sat down next to me a minute later. He's the *Cove's* supplier for what fish they can't get directly from the charter boats, and he trucks it over from his depot in Hampton. A nice enough guy, and generally pretty quiet. Today was no exception, as he had picked up the latest ESVA Telegraph, our local and free weekly newspaper. He was silently catching up on the recent news, as it had been delivered this morning.

"Son of a bit... er, sorry ma'am," he said to Lindsay about almost completing the curse. He pointed to the paper, "But I know this guy! I picked him up off the road on Fisherman Island early Monday morning a few hours before sunrise. Said he had been hitchhiking and some jerk stopped and dumped him there. I gave him a ride up to Melfa."

I looked over to where he was pointing. There on the front page was a picture of Marty Stoneman.

20

"I AM GEORGE!"

I called and got Chuck Canfield's number from Casey, who had his card in his wallet. The deputy came racing into the restaurant's office where we had taken Andy so that others wouldn't overhear their conversation. Mimi was out working the floor, so the room was empty. With Marty apparently still alive, we all figured it would be to law enforcement's advantage not to let anyone else know, at least for now.

Canfield listened to Andy recount his encounter with Stoneman, and how he thought at the time it was strange that his clothes seemed a bit damp. As cold as it was that morning, Marty had been shivering uncontrollably when he got into the cab. Andy had turned up the cab's heater until he stopped shaking. By the time they reached Melfa, his clothes were mostly dry.

All that Andy could get out of him was that his name was George, and he was on his way to Melfa. Other than that, and telling him the story about being dumped on Fisherman Island, he said very little. Andy had hoped he'd be someone to talk to in order to pass the time, but he hadn't counted on having to carry most of the conversation himself since it wasn't in his nature. It didn't take long before he gave up trying.

Canfield said, "Stoneman's middle name is George. He must've been trying to not be completely deceptive while not telling you the full truth. But he is still willing to let everyone think he drowned."

"And that his sister had possibly killed him," I added.

"Any idea where she might be?"

Lindsay said, "We haven't seen her today, but ESVA Security has someone with her. I'll call and find out." She hit her speed dial for Rikki and had a brief conversation. "She said Sandra had an appointment this morning at the funeral home, and she thinks they are headed back here after that. She's calling her associate to find out exactly where they are."

"Do you need me anymore? This lunch has taken longer than I thought, and I've got other deliveries to make," Andy said.

Canfield let him leave after taking his cell phone number and making him promise not to tell anyone anything about his encounter with Stoneman.

Lindsay's phone rang. After she answered, she looked very concerned. She hung up and said, "Rikki's associate isn't answering. His phone isn't showing up on their locator. She's sending some of her people down to the funeral home to check."

"I'm on the way there. Remember, not a word about Stoneman," Canfield admonished us.

After he left, I of course called Rikki back immediately and told her the full story. No matter what Canfield said, her people needed to know what they are up against, and who to look out for. At the very least, Marty is a disturbed person. At worst, he might be a murderer, and possibly even a double murderer. If he is, hopefully, he hasn't added another couple of bodies to his list.

Just in case, Lindsay and I checked the parking lot over near *Privacy* for a black Escalade that is ESVA Security's standard-issue vehicle for protection jobs. But as we suspected, there wasn't one in sight. We went to *OCT* to change, then it was back to our original plan to go work on *LNZ II*. As much as I'd love to help find Marty, it was best left to the pros.

Rikki did call a couple of hours later to let us know her associate had been found, alive but woozy and stuffed in the trunk of an old, classic Chevelle in the parking lot of the funeral home. He said he never got a clear look at his attacker before he was tazed, and then a rag was shoved in his face with a sweet-smelling chemical, likely chloroform.

When he regained consciousness, he was in the car's trunk, and his nine-millimeter Glock pistol was missing along with his phone. The phone was found on the asphalt behind the car, smashed. They had traced the Chevelle back to Martin Stoneman, Senior. It had been the Mole's father's car. But there was no trace of the Escalade, Sandra Stoneman, or her brother. She had kept her appointment and then left, though none of the funeral home people could recall seeing her get into a car or talk with anyone outside.

While I'm glad that Rik's associate was safe, now I feared the worst had already happened to Sandra Stoneman.

THE ROOM WAS SPINNING, and Sandra felt nauseated, very close to throwing up. Through sheer willpower, she managed to overcome nausea in a few minutes, and the room was slowly coming to a stop. She was in a sitting position, propped up against one of the wheels of the black SUV. Her hands were tied behind her back, and her ankles were bound together. What she could see of the large room was that it was constructed entirely of poured concrete, with an industrial rollup door on one end.

"Well, well, back among the living, are we?"

She focused on where the familiar-sounding voice had originated and tried to cover her shock with bravado.

"I never pictured heaven as being made of concrete."

"HOW DARE YOU SPEAK OF HEAVEN!" Marty screamed. "YOU HAVE NO CHANCE OF EVER GOING THERE UNLESS YOU REPENT!"

She was taken aback for a moment as the room began to spin again. Then she gathered her courage to confront him.

"I am the one who needs to repent, brother? You're the one who is holding me here against my will! And what about the murders of our father and Reverend Branson? Was that all your doing as well?"

"Do NOT call that evil man a *'reverend'* as he was an impostor, a FRAUD! There was no saving him; nothing but evil lurked in his heart. I merely let the evil out of him. It leaped out, all red and wet, wanting to be out of his body.

"As for our father, he made his choice long ago; he defiled the Scriptures for his greed, stealing from the very people he was supposed to be leading and protecting. He should have been setting an example for them, helping them to get closer to God. Instead, he only wanted to be closer to whatever little money they had. There was no saving him either. Nothing but greed dwelled within his heart, his very soul had died along with our mother's. When people become that way on their own, there is nothing that can be done. Their evil also needs to be extinguished and cast out of this world. The ironic thing is that one of God's most beautiful creations, the oleander flower, was what sent our father on his way.

"But you, my sister, you can still be saved. You need merely to repent and denounce the evil of your so-called 'prosperity gospel.' Believing in this heresy is not your fault. Our father brainwashed you at such a young and impressionable age, making you believe his own bastardized descriptions of the holiest writings in our world. Your soul was being sucked from you by him, and that was part of why he had to die.

"But I KNOW you can still be saved. Give up the ways of our father and accept the Word of the one true God! The one who reigns over all, the one who used me as His tool to rid the world of two that would never turn away from their continuing evil, greedy ways. The one who has shown me that you CAN be saved, that you ARE worth saving. That you can truly do good from this point on, to give back to those from whom you have taken. To accept the Word as it was written, not as it was twisted by our father.

"When you can recite the true meaning of each passage, I will free you to let you begin to repair the damage that you have done. Until then, we will stay here together, and you will learn."

Sandra looked at her brother with a combination of fear and pity. "Martin, just let me go, and I'll get you some help…"

"NO! IT IS YOU THAT NEEDS THE HELP, THAT NEEDS TO BE SAVED! AND NEVER CALL ME BY THAT MAN'S FIRST NAME AGAIN! I AM GEORGE!" With that, he stormed off somewhere out of sight beyond the SUV.

THE CUDDY CABIN UP forward was the biggest mess, with black mold having formed everywhere in the long-closed space. Lindsay tackled that while I scrubbed and cleaned the open cockpit. Two of Carlton's mechanics were busy hanging the engines, hooking up the controls, and cleaning out the old gas tank.

There was a large, open hole in the center console where a touch-screen display had once been and four holes in the hardtop where a radar unit had been mounted. We planned to get *LNZ II* all cleaned up and over to Casey's Cove tomorrow morning. After she's over there, we'll worry about installing new electronics. I was just as glad that it was all gone since it meant I got a better price for the hull, and we'll be going back in with the latest gear. There's nothing worse than paying top dollar for someone's old, shaky, and outdated electronics.

"Whew!" Lindsay emerged from the cuddy, pulling off a painter's respirator mask. "If the liquid chlorine doesn't kill it all, the fumes will. Hey, the deck came up nice!"

"I knew it would. We'll still end up painting it at some point with polyurethane and nonskid, but I want to get her in the water and run her a bit first. Besides, she's an older boat who's going to work for a living, not be a showpiece like her older Merritt brother."

"Hey! It's not nice to talk about a lady's age, Babe!" Lindsay grinned, already getting attached to the new rig.

Wait until she sees how this one runs; these thirty-ones ride a bit bow-high making them comfortable in a chop. The tradeoff is they're a little wet, but nothing that some wrap-around isinglass on the hardtop frame can't handle. That's an accessory also known as a removable "telephone booth." Marlin has the same setup on his Gold Line outboard.

"Lady? She's no lady, she's a tough old broad!"

"Well, we're going to treat her like a young lady."

Uh, oh. I wanted an older rig that I wasn't so worried about running hard when I need to. Sounds like Lindsay is already getting protective of this one.

"Pretty classy for a workboat." Casey had stopped by and was peering over the gunwale. He had climbed up on the stepladder we were using to get on and off the boat while it was in the boatyard, "up on the hard."

Lindsay cocked her head slightly and put her hands on her hips, "See? Casey agrees with me!"

"Whoa! I didn't drop by to get in the middle of you two, I just wanted to see what you bought. So far, I'm impressed."

I said, "I hope you stay that way after we get her in the water."

"I'm thinking that won't be a problem. When are you going to splash her?"

"Tomorrow morning sometime."

"I'll be here. I'll even drive you two up here, so you don't have to shuffle cars." He climbed in and looked around. Spotting the large hole, he said, "Air-conditioned console?"

I replied, "Fiberglass termites."

"At least they didn't tear it up too badly getting the electronics stripped out of it."

"Yeah, considerate thieves. Regular Virginia gentlemen." While theft around the Virginia waterfront is an issue, it is only a fraction of the size of the problem that exists in our old native home of South Florida. It's not often down there that things are removed so surgically, and repairing the damage left behind can sometimes cost as much as replacing the pilfered electronics.

Looking aft he remarked, "Twin two-fifties, nice! What are you expecting out of her for speed?" Casey asked.

"Somewhere around fifty mph at wide-open-throttle, and a good thirty-plus at cruise. A lot of these thirty-ones have twin three-hundreds, and a few have even gone up to twin fours. But at her age, it's better to go low and slow, rather than stress her out."

He nodded. "Engines have gotten so big now, these two-fifties are babies. I remember not that long ago when they were considered huge."

Lindsay said, "And the boats equipped with engines this size will probably still be around in twenty more years. The ones that now have four six-hundred horsepower V-12s, I question how long those will last."

The size of outboard motors has been increasing at a fast pace over the last few years, as has the length of the boats they are being mounted on. Nobody knows where it's going to stop. As for me, I'm more of an inboard fan for boats larger than this one. Thirty years ago, the sixty-footers were considered large, but they were also a common size for a sport fisherman. Today, ninety and even a hundred feet is quickly becoming the norm for the modern fishing "battlewagon."

I guess I'm old-fashioned; I like this particular center console rig. It's just a few years younger than Linds. A basic fishing machine, unlike today's models with all their added crap. More junk to break and need continual maintenance. No thanks, I'm a big fan of simple.

Casey said, "Well, this one looks pretty good, except for the cosmetics. I'm looking forward to seeing how she performs tomorrow."

"Yeah, so are we," I replied.

"You two have to be freezing, the water coming out of that hose must be like ice." He pointed to my water-shriveled fingers.

Lindsay said, "We're almost done. If Murph would quit bogarting the hose, I can rinse the cuddy cabin then we can go home and warm up."

I passed her the business end of the hose, and she went back to work. I turned to Casey, "Hear anything more from Rikki?"

"Nothing yet. Since Marty was headed to Melfa, I'm guessing he must've had a garage up there where he had that Chevelle stashed, and maybe a house with it. They could be anywhere on the Shore, and not necessarily in Virginia. If Stoneman has that Escalade inside a garage, it'll be next to impossible to find."

I speculated, "He's avoided the cops so far, and if it hadn't been for us running into Andy, we'd still think he drowned. But you're right, he could be anywhere on the Shore. For her sake, I hope his sister is still alive. I feel like she probably is since he left Branson's body behind, and he poisoned his father where he was sure to be found. If he had already killed her, they'd have probably found the body by now."

∽

THE NEXT MORNING...

"WAKE UP, my sister. Time to start class again."

Sandra pulled herself to a sitting position. The handcuffs that bound her wrists were chained to a metal support column next to the Escalade.

"As if I could really sleep on this thing," she indicated the thin piece of egg crate foam under her. "And I need to go to the bathroom."

Marty brandished the taser he had used to subdue both her and the driver.

"Okay, but no tricks. This concrete floor wouldn't be as forgiving as that car seat was yesterday if you were to fall."

He led her to a small bathroom with no windows and removed her handcuffs long enough for her to use the facilities. Then he brought her back over to the same two chairs they had sat in yesterday. They had spent hour after hour there while he tried to get her to renounce the "prosperity gospel" view of the Scriptures.

Originally, she considered faking changing her position over to his viewpoint, but she knew he would expect her to be resistant. So, she planned on continuing today, and then eventually allow him to persuade her to see things his way. The tricky part was in figuring out when. Give in too fast, and he'd see through it. Wait too long, and he'd tire of his attempts.

She knew he had already killed their father and Branson, and she had no illusions about her meeting the same fate if he was pushed beyond a certain point. There was little doubt that he was now totally, and certifiably, insane. Some kind of psychotic break she guessed, though she was far from an expert on it.

"Right, let's get started." He began reading aloud in a monotone, and she feigned interest in what he was saying, like a participant in a high school debate.

I DIDN'T SLEEP WELL. Not because I wasn't tired, but more because I was like a little kid on Christmas Eve. I wanted to get over to Carlton's and play with my new toy. It's funny, you would think that the performance characteristics of identical production boats would be just that, identical. Not so. There are always little subtle differences, even between boats that come out of the same molds. I've ridden on a few thirty-one Contenders, so I know pretty much what to expect. But I'm anxious to get some helm time today and get to know my new "gal" better.

I whipped up breakfast for the two of us in the galley. After cleaning up afterward, I made four coffees "to go" for us, Casey, and Dawn. I knew Dawn wouldn't want to miss the launch. I grabbed a handheld VHF radio from its charger since the one that had been on the boat had also been stolen.

Dawn actually turned out to be our driver this morning. She and

Casey were waiting in her idling Escalade when we emerged from *OCT*.

"Morning, kids!" Lindsay said as we climbed into the backseats, handing our spare coffees forward.

"Ready for the splash?" Dawn asked.

"Even more ready for what comes afterward. I'm dying to run our new baby," Linds gushed.

Wait, wasn't I the one who originally wanted to buy an outboard? Yeah, from the sound of it, I'm thinking I'll be lucky if I get any helm time at all. And I had thought *I* was the excited one. Casey turned around and looked at me, silently chuckling, and I frowned back at him in a mute reply.

It was a busy morning. Lorry from Lorry's Lettering came by and installed the custom vinyl lettering with the name and hailing port amidships, and the state registration numbers up on the bow. Then Chief's Canvas, one of the businesses in the building that also houses ESVAcats, sent someone over to measure for the "telephone booth." While this was going on, Carlton's guys fired up the engines using a water hose for cooling while they checked everything out. Finally, the strap lift picked up the hull and rolled us over to the launching slip. The operator lowered *LNZ II*'s bow down until it was level with the seawall and about a foot away, allowing Lindsay and me to easily step aboard. A minute later, we were floating.

I know what you're thinking, and the answer is "no." As in I wasn't the one that backed her out of the slip and negotiated the channel through the marsh flats and out into Magothy Bay. Lindsay had grabbed the wheel as soon as we were aboard. But you know, there's something so damn sexy about a confident woman at the helm of a boat.

Lindsay's blonde hair was tied in a braid to keep it from tangling, she had on a green Mallard Cove ball cap and aviator sunglasses. We both wore jeans and lined jackets to counter the chilly, almost winter-like air.

I did mention that she looked sexy, right?

"Penny for your thoughts, Babe!" She was grinning, and I guess I was about as tough to read as a billboard. "But I still want to put more hours on her first. Though tonight might be perfect hot tub weather if you play your cards right."

I'm pretty sure she winked behind those sunglasses. And what the heck, there will be plenty of time for me to run the boat later. In the meantime, I had the best-looking captain on Magothy Bay.

21

―――――

CRUISE TO HELL

Casey and Dawn met us at the fuel dock, we had only put enough fuel onboard at Carlton's to get us back to *Mallard Cove*. Almost three hundred gallons later, *LNZ II* was full. Another thing I liked about this boat was she had the optional larger tanks. I just hoped I'd get a turn at the wheel at some point before we need to refuel.

Lindsay addressed Dawn as she boarded, "She runs like a dream! Wait until this summer, Dawn, she'll be perfect for the two of us to run out to the canyons and fish together." The canyons are the summer fishing hot spots, about sixty miles off the coast. Dawn joined Lindsay on the lean seat behind the helm, leaving Casey and me to handle the dock lines and perch on the only remaining seat, the one in front of the console.

"I'm game! Maybe we can get Kari and Missy to go some, too," Dawn replied.

Okay, now I hoped I'd get a chance to drive at some point before *then*. I probably should've named the dang thing "*MRF II*" just to assert a little ownership. Linds pointed our bow out the basin's inlet, then she sped up to wide-open-throttle after we were clear of the rock jetties. With our

178

engines already having been "broken in" by their original owner, we didn't have to worry about going slow. And Lindsay was bringing new meaning to the saying, "drive it like you stole it." Because in a way, she did.

Casey glanced back, then turned to look at me. He was laughing. I looked back and saw what he thought was so funny. Dawn was now at the helm, having gotten to run my new boat before me. At least I think it's my boat. I glared at him again, which made him laugh even harder.

As we passed under Fisherman Inlet Bridge and out into the Chesapeake, Dawn started a slow turn to starboard, straightening out when we were headed up the bay.

"Where are we going?" I yelled to be heard above the engines and fifty miles-per-hour of wind.

Lindsay yelled back, "You guys are taking us to lunch at *Bayside,* then we're going to Gwynn's Island, and back home." She started throttling back to cruising speed.

"Do I get to run my boat at any point today?"

"Probably not!" She was grinning widely.

AFTER A GREAT LUNCH at the *Bayside Club,* we set out again, this time in a three-foot head sea. This is usually the worst angle for this particular model of boat, but the waves were so close together we literally skipped across them with very little pounding. And thankfully with very little spray. While these were far from the biggest waves we'll ever encounter coming back and forth across the bay, I was still very pleased with the Contender's performance so far.

Larry Donnelly, the realtor, met us at the dock. Like the last time we were here, he told us to take our time looking through the buildings. We gave the place another very thorough, close-up inspection, and our worst fears were confirmed. Just about everything that had been done by "the reverends" crews would now have to be redone; it was all substandard work. But at the price we are paying, we could afford to get it done right this time.

We spent most of the afternoon on the property since this was the first time Casey and Dawn had seen it in person.

"You were right on the money about this place having possibilities. Nice catch, you two," Dawn said.

Casey nodded and said, "I'm particularly looking forward to running up against Cetta again." Glenn Cetta had been in the middle of our deal at Cape Charles and had caused Casey a lot of trouble. Paybacks are sweet at times. Like now. Up until this point, Cetta's property has been the "go-to" spot around here for waterfront weddings, having the most venues on a single property. Now we'll tie him. Oh, to be a fly on the wall when he hears about what we're up to.

I nodded, "I can't wait, either."

We got back aboard after saying goodbye to Larry. Once again, Lindsay was back at the helm and took us under the bridge and through the harbor.

"Well, since we had to buy lunch, you two are buying us dinner at the *Cove*," Casey stated.

"Especially since neither of us has gotten to run this rig," I griped. Now it was more like a game of "keep away," and the women had the ball. To be honest, though, I was glad that Lindsay liked the boat and was planning to use it with her girlfriends.

Lindsay pulled into the dock in the corner of the marina basin over by the outdoor cook shack. This dock is reserved for our restaurant customers. Normally it stays packed in the summer, but now we were the only boat tied up here since the cold weather meant the season was over. The shack is now closed until the opening of crab season in early spring. Then it'll be running nonstop from before noon until closing every day, supplying steamed and charcoal-grilled seafood to the two beach bars as well as the *Cove*.

It was almost dark when we stepped onto the dock, the fall time change having happened not that long ago. We hustled into the restaurant to warm up. As we sat at our table, I looked around at my three friends, all with the same windburned glow on their faces that I was feeling. It had been a banner day, and I didn't know what I was most pleased about, that *LNZ II* had turned out so well, or that Casey and Dawn liked the new project as much as we did.

This was now the second property that Lindsay and I had found which had turned out to be a winner for our investment group. I've learned just about everything I know about real estate from Casey. His knowing that I can spot a good deal and having him trust my judgment is a huge feeling of accomplishment for me. Don't forget, just under twenty years ago I went to work for him part-time, keeping his boat washed. Now he considers me an equal, something that I'm very proud of.

I guess I was being extra quiet this evening, letting the other three carry the conversation. Lindsay must've suddenly realized this, and she gave me a concerned look. I smiled and winked at her, and she relaxed a bit, though she did give me a few furtive glances throughout the rest of the meal.

On the way back out to the boat, Lindsay handed me the keys, giggling as she did.

"Here you go, Babe, you wanted to run our boat."

"Oh, gee, thanks. I get to go all of a few hundred yards, and you two ran it a hundred miles."

"It wasn't that far! Okay, maybe it *was* close to that, but there will be lots more of those runs in the future."

I backed out of the slip, and spun us around, heading for the inlet. But something wasn't right. Not with our boat, but with the marina, and I couldn't put my finger on it. Then it hit me; *Privacy* was missing. With her new owner also missing, Gary Stevens would have never moved her. Unless Sandra Stoneman had been found, something was very, very wrong. I steered over to the dock where Privacy's shore power cord lay all coiled up and waiting for her return, meaning this wasn't a permanent move.

Casey, Dawn, and Lindsay never said a word, all having realized what I had. Then I looked down the dock and what I spotted in the parking lot gave me chills. A blacked-out Escalade like the one ESVA Security was missing. I still had Gary Stevens' number on my phone.

It went straight to voicemail. Then I pulled out my handheld VHF from under the lean seat and tried hailing him, but with no luck. I called Rikki and put the call on speaker. She said no, neither they nor the sheriff's office had located either the missing SUV or Sandra Stoneman.

While I was talking to Rik, I opened the Automatic Identification System (AIS) app on my phone. Larger private and all commercial boats are required to be equipped with a transponder that gives their name, heading, speed, and other details. *Privacy* popped up, three miles out and heading southeast at four knots.

"Well, there's a black Escalade here that looks like yours, and *Privacy* has left the marina, heading southeast. Captain Stevens isn't answering his phone or the VHF."

She replied, "That's not good. Whoever kidnapped Sandra Stoneman must've hijacked the boat."

I said, "I'm betting that he or she has her with them. No way Gary would've taken that boat out on his own without the owner's permission, he's too much of a pro for that."

"Agreed. I'll call the sheriff and the coast guard."

"Wait, Rik. I got Gary into this in the first place by hooking him up with Stoneman, and then I talked him into staying with them. I feel responsible for getting him into whatever 'this' turns out to be. Casey, Dawn, Linds, and I are all armed. We'll have a much better chance of getting in close to see what's going on than the Coasties would with their blue lights flashing and their easily identifiable boats. We look more like a boat just heading out to do some night fishing offshore." Though I hoped no one aboard would notice our lack of fishing rods if they spotted us.

Rik knows I've gotten aboard moving boats before, and they were going at a much faster speed. We might have a shot at it again if we need to, and if *Privacy* keeps going this slow.

"I don't like this, but okay. Only you make sure that you keep in contact with me. I want to be kept up on what's happening. Meanwhile, I'm heading down to Mallard Cove to check out that SUV."

I said, "We both know the reason you don't like this is because you aren't here to go with us."

She sighed, "Pretty much. Don't get shot at this time."

"I'll do my best, *mom*."

"Smartass. All you guys be careful."

"Roger that." I hung up, steered us through the inlet then fire-walled the throttles, racing out into the dark water beyond. Asking the others if they were up for this wasn't necessary, I already knew their answers.

I shut off our running lights. This did two things: it lets me see the water around us better without any reflection from them and kept us from being spotted by any lookout on *Privacy*. There was plenty of light coming from the far-off glow of VA Beach that would backlight any other boat traffic around us. But oh, how I'd love to have a working radar right about now.

"My dear sister, you are a smart one. I'm glad that you've come to see things properly. But you may be too smart, so we're going to have a little test. One that I've already taken myself and passed. If you have truly had a change of heart, you won't have any problem passing it either. So, I need you to call our captain, his number is on the top of this pad. And you need to tell him what I've written out for you."

He handed her a legal pad and a disposable cell phone. That's when she noticed that he had swapped the taser for a Glock semi-automatic pistol. Playtime was over. If he believed she had indeed come over to his way of thinking, she had nothing to fear. But if he didn't, he wasn't about to waste any more time on her.

"Captain Stevens, this is Sandra Stoneman... yes, yes, I'm fine, thanks to the good Lord. I'll tell you everything when I see you. But right now, I need you to do something for me, and you have to keep it in the strictest confidence. Please pick your two most trusted crewmen, because the police want me to go anchor out for a bit. They said that on the boat is the safest place I can be right now... yes, probably only a day or two, three at most. But when you call your crewmen, you have to swear them to secrecy. My life may well depend on your discretion... Thank you, I'll see you shortly." She hung up the phone and looked at Marty. "Did I pass?"

"What? Oh, that wasn't the test. At least not the big part. That'll be coming up. Give me your hands." He unlocked the handcuffs. "This is how much I trust you now. But you don't want to violate that trust." He shoved the Glock in his waistband. "Get in the front passenger seat."

Sandra did as she was told as he donned a pair of thin leather gloves and climbed into the driver's seat. Marty hit a button on a small remote and the garage door opened, then he passed her a ballcap.

"Here, put this on." She thought it was overkill, since they were in a vehicle with limousine tinting on the windows, and she could see through the doorway that it was dusk. But he was the one with the gun, and she wasn't about to argue with him.

A little over thirty minutes later they pulled into *Mallard Cove*, and he parked near *Privacy*'s dock. He zippered his windbreaker and raised the hood over his head, then pulled the Glock from his waistband and shoved it in the windbreaker's side pocket. He had his hand on the grip still.

"Let's go. This is all part of the test my sister, and this is one you don't want to flunk because I don't grade on a curve." He smiled at her. "Make sure to keep your face down so you aren't spotted by anyone."

They walked down the dock side by side, and she kept her head down as instructed. *Privacy* was ready to go, and the crewmen were standing by to cast off the dock lines. The gangway had already been stowed and the shore power cord disconnected. *Privacy*'s generators were now running and carrying the load. They stepped aboard on the aft boarding/swim platform, then climbed one of the side spiral stairs up to the aft deck, making their way through the salon and up to the raised pilothouse. There they found Gary Stevens. He was shocked to see Marty, who had now pulled back his hood. He was even more shocked to see the pistol he was holding.

"Hello, captain. Nice to see you again. As soon as we cast off, I want you to call your crewmen up here. If everyone does as they're told, we'll all make it back to land, safe and sound, and there'll be a bonus in it for all of you."

"But... you went overboard! We all thought you drowned."

"I'm sorry about deceiving you, but I had some things I had to do for God, and I needed everyone to think I was dead to accomplish those. I used a knife to draw some blood and yanked a few hairs to add to it to make it look like I fell and hit my head."

Sandra knew he had left her to take the blame on purpose. She also knew that insane or not, there was no way that he was going to leave her or their crew alive to identify him as being the hijacker.

Marty said, "Now get us out of here, and no tricks on that headset while you're talking with your crew. Remember, you need to call them up here as soon as we're off the dock. Once we clear the shallows, I want you to steer one-four-five degrees."

Gary nodded slowly, acknowledging the southeast course instruction despite realizing that all was not right with this situation. However, he also knew that there would be strength in numbers. Having his crewmen up on the pilothouse bridge with him would divide Marty's attention, and give them better odds if they got a chance to rush him. He wasn't certain yet if Sandra was a willing part of whatever this was or not.

"Okay, cast off aft, cast off forward." Gary used both the bow and stern thrusters simultaneously to move Privacy sideways off the dock, then he shut off the stern, letting the bow thruster continue to swing the bow out farther, lining them up with the basin's inlet. He dimmed the bridge lights.

"Why did you do that? Turn those lights back up!" Marty was becoming alarmed.

"Dimming the bridge lights allows me to see out through the glass better. It's tight in this inlet."

"Alright, but once we're out in open water, turn them back up.

You've got two radars and other stuff to navigate with, right? I'm more concerned with being able to see everything that's going on in here."

Once they were out past the jetties, Marty reminded him, "Now call the rest of the crew up here and turn those lights back up."

After Gary complied, Marty moved over to a corner of the bridge where he wouldn't be spotted before the other crewmen were out of the stairwell and onto the bridge deck. Both of them arrived and moved toward Gary but froze once they spotted Marty. Each looked like they were seeing a ghost, and then they saw the pistol.

"Gentlemen, thank you for coming. Now if you will just hand over your cell phones to my sister, oh, and please collect the captain's as well."

Sandra said, "Marty, you don't have to do this."

"I TOLD YOU MY NAME IS GEORGE! NOW TAKE THEIR PHONES AND HAND THEM TO ME!" he shouted.

Sandra did as he was told, and he pulled three sets of handcuffs out of his windbreaker pocket and then handed them to her.

"Cuff those two to the railing on the stairs." He motioned menacingly at the two crewmen with the Glock. "Gentlemen, this is for your protection. Some things need doing that you might not understand at first, but you will later, and then there will be large bonuses waiting for you ashore after we are through. Sandra, cuff the captain's one arm to the helm chair as well."

Sandra moved over to Gary, looking at him apologetically. Then she loosely cuffed one wrist to an armrest support.

"Uh, sister, don't you think that's a little loose? We wouldn't want him getting free before your big test now, would we?"

She tightened the cuff several more notches.

"Captain, aren't we going a lot slower than that night I went for a swim? How about speeding it up a bit."

"I wouldn't advise it unless you want us to sink or lose our running gear. The Coast Guard issued a warning this afternoon that an inbound cargo ship had lost several dozen shipping containers overboard. Many are reported to be floating at surface level around here. No way to see them at night before we hit them. Going any faster than this could risk us hitting one, getting holed, and then sinking. That's not something I want to happen since I'm chained to it." He glared at Marty, who either didn't notice or didn't care. The truth is there was no container ship. But wherever they were headed, Gary wasn't in a hurry to get there because he was sure that when they did, something bad was going to happen. There was no doubt in his mind that Marty was completely insane. Then his phone went off in Marty's pocket, startling him and almost causing him to pull the trigger on the Glock, which has no safety.

Marty pulled the phone out and silenced the call. A minute later the VHF squawked, "Motoryacht *Privacy*, fishing vessel *LNZ II*, do you read me, cap?"

"Who is this *LNZ II*," Marty demanded to know.

"I've never heard of it before," Gary answered truthfully. "Maybe we waked out somebody who's at anchor, and they're mad." While he didn't know a boat by that name, he recognized Murph's voice. He must've seen that *Privacy* had left and known something wasn't kosher. Now hopefully he would send help, and whoever it is, the captain silently prayed they would be stealthy. There was little doubt now that both his and his crew's lives depended on that.

22

DEAD AHEAD

"I've got 'em, dead ahead," Casey said.

"Don't use the word 'dead,' Case," I asked.

We could see the white stern light on *Privacy*'s stern. The three-foot following sea wasn't affecting her at all, as the light stayed level and steady.

Lindsay said, "Looks like they're just over idle speed."

I said, "Let's hope they stay that way. I'm going to run past 'em and see if we can spot anyone aboard."

I throttled us back to cruising speed and planned on passing about thirty yards off their port beam. This should keep us outside of any light spilling from the yacht, and with our lights off and a moonless night, we should be invisible to them except on their radar. We aren't equipped with an Automatic Identification System (AIS), so they wouldn't be able to identify us if we were spotted.

Two minutes later I was surprised to see so much light coming from the raised pilothouse, but that paled to my surprise at seeing who I was inside it. It was official, Marty Stoneman was back from the dead. As soon as I spotted him, I altered my course sixty degrees to port, aiming offshore. I don't think we were spotted, but if we were, it looks like we're now headed out to the canyons.

188

. . .

THE MAIN BRIDGE in the raised pilothouse has five large flatscreen displays. All can show anything from various video cameras placed around the yacht to the Forward Looking Infrared (FLIR), both the short and long-range radars, engine gauges, and systems. Gary had been concentrating on their short-range radar on one of them ever since he heard that radio call. Covering only the three miles around their boat, it barely reached back to *Mallard Cove*. There was only one target on it right now off their stern, it had left *Mallard Cove* and made a beeline straight for them.

While Marty was focused on his sister, Gary dropped out the three-mile radar on that display and replaced it with their forty-eight-mile one. There were a few dozen targets out ahead and moving about on the screen, making that sole one behind them less noticeable except to him. He turned off the proximity alarm that would've gone off if the approaching boat had come within a quarter-mile because he hoped that it would.

Gary gave the screen occasional, almost disinterested glances, but he was happy to see that target come up abeam of them and then head out to sea. If it was indeed Murph, this is exactly what he would expect him to do. Gary glanced out the port window, but with all the lights now on in the pilothouse, he wasn't able to see out through the reflection. He was sure that whoever was on that boat had been able to see in, however. Another glance showed that the boat had now turned back toward the marina.

Marty had switched into what Gary took to be his preaching voice, meaning he was now demanding their attention. He was saying something about a test of faith and true repentance, and that the time now had come.

Gary glanced back to the screen again and saw the target had now moved in behind them and was closing the distance. It had to be Murph. Please, let it be Murph.

. . .

AFTER RUNNING toward the canyons for two minutes I made a wide circle to port until I finally ended up directly astern of *Privacy* and several hundred yards behind her.

I said, "Okay Linds, you take the helm. At her slow speed, it shouldn't be too turbulent behind the swim platform. You'll need to get up within a foot of it and match their speed exactly. Then Case and I will step across from our bow. You'll need to watch us closely, if one of us slips, you'll need to go into neutral 'like yesterday' to keep us from getting chopped up by our wheels."

"I'm going with you guys," Dawn said.

"Negative. I need you on here as a pair of extra eyes and hands for Lindsay. If things get hairy, we may have to jump overboard. That water's only around fifty degrees. If you guys don't pick us up right away, we'll only be able to tread water for maybe fifteen minutes before we start losing muscle control. If you miss seeing us go over the side, we won't make it to shore from here."

Casey said, "Murph's right. We'll be fine, Dawn. But you two need to drop back far enough so you don't get illuminated by their stern light. Plus, then you'll be able to see down both sides of their boat."

"You be careful." Lindsay grabbed my arm then pulled me to her and kissed me.

"Trust me."

GARY WATCHED HELPLESSLY as Marty led Sandra down the pilothouse stairs to the side deck entry door. Through the chrome railing, Gary could see what was about to happen, but he was powerless to stop it. At gunpoint, Marty made Sandra slide the glass door open, then open the gunwale boarding door. He heard him tell her that he had survived the cold water because it was part of God's plan, and if she has truly turned away from the prosperity gospel, he would save her now as well.

Gary knew that if she went into that water, she was done for. There was no way she could survive long enough to reach shore before hypothermia set in. As the yacht's captain, he was responsible for her life.

He yelled, "Hey, you sick son of a bitch, leave her alone! She'll die if she goes overboard."

A red-hot poker jabbed him in his side, and he fell to the deck, his one hand restrained up by the armrest of the helm seat. Even twenty feet away, the sound of the Glock was deafening on the bridge. Gary moaned in agony and his two crewmen were helpless, unable to reach him because of their own restraints. But now they knew for certain what their fate would be at the hands of this madman.

"Marty, STOP!" Sandra lunged for the gun, grabbing it with both hands. It went off, and she tumbled over backward into the dark water, her look of shock and surprise etching itself into his memory.

"For the last time, my name is George. And I knew you wouldn't pass the test."

AT THIS SPEED, the Contender rode at an angle that put its bow even with the top of the removable stainless safety rails on the yacht's swim platform. Lindsay's experience with the new boat came into play as she matched *Privacy*'s speed perfectly, holding us steady a mere six inches from the rails. This allowed Casey and me to easily leap down to the platform's teak deck. Lindsay then chopped the throttles, and *LNZ II* dropped back into the darkness.

Casey took the starboard curved stairs while I took the port, making our way up to the dark aft deck, which was deserted. The salon was just beyond a glass bulkhead with a pair of stainless framed glass doors. All the lights in the salon were on. Down the companionway, we spotted Marty taking Sandra out through the port side entry door. Once they were out of sight, we went into the salon and heard Gary yelling before a gunshot rang out. A few seconds later, we heard another shot, and Marty started back through the door. By that point, Casey and I were out in the open in the middle of the salon, with no cover and about a quarter-second away from being spotted. I did the only thing I could do, and I took a shot at Marty while we both were moving.

The bullet missed Marty and buried itself into the doorway. He ducked back out through the door as Casey and I dove to either side of the salon. Marty stuck his hand with the gun through the doorway and started firing blind. The glass bulkhead and doors behind us shattered as he sprayed the room with bullets.

At first, the only part of Marty I could see was his hand. Then I caught a glimpse of him running up the side deck toward the bow. I motioned to Casey to go out the starboard side door while I followed Marty out the port. Sticking my head out the door for a split second, I saw him aiming back my way. I ducked back in as two bullets flew past where my head had been.

I yelled out the door, "Marty! Drop the gun and let's talk."

Another gunshot. "MY NAME IS GEORGE! YOU CAN'T HARM ME; GOD WON'T ALLOW IT!"

"Mar... George, put down the gun, and let's talk."

"Why don't you come out here first! TALK TO THIS!" Another gunshot.

"George, I don't want to hurt you."

"LIAR! YOU WERE SENT HERE BY SATAN TO STOP ME, BUT I'M GOING TO STOP YOU INSTEAD! ARRRRRRR!"

He was racing down the side deck, coming at me, and I backed up the companionway into the salon, taking cover behind the dining area bulkhead corner. I stooped down, peering around as I heard several shots outside. Marty made it partway into the door when I started shooting, and these were mostly center-mass hits. His eyes went wide, he dropped the Glock as he stumbled backward, falling through the same open boarding door his sister had gone through moments before.

Casey appeared, first looking overboard, then walking into the salon.

"You good?"

I nodded. "I've probably got you to thank for that. Looked like you winged him before I finished him off."

"*Winged* him? He was a dead man walking; he just hadn't figured that part out yet. I nailed him several times."

I went out on the back deck, turning on the lights so Lindsay could see me. I called her phone.

"Hey, did you see Sandra go overboard?"

She sounded harried, "We have her in the boat, gunshot wound, and it's bad."

"Haul ass, I'll call Rikki! You'll probably be there before any ambulance." I saw running lights switch on a hundred yards behind us, the forward red light disappearing as she made her turn. I watched the white stern light that replaced it recede into the darkness. I dialed Rikki and told her what happened, and then I heard Casey yelling.

"Murph, get your butt up here, I need help!"

I double-timed it to the pilothouse stairs. When I reached the top, it was bad. Casey was holding pressure on Gary's wound, and there was a lot of blood on the deck. Seeing that both other crewmen were handcuffed to the railing, they weren't going to be a lot of help unless there was a key around. They confirmed there wasn't. I had sent the only fast boat we had to shore, not that I could've freed Gary to get him on it.

I got behind the wheel, firewalled both engines, and made as tight a one-eighty as this big pig would turn. At least we were a little over half the speed of the Contender, and we'd make the marina in well under ten minutes. I called Rikki back and explained our situation.

"You just get him here; I can get the cuffs open," she said.

"I've got some quick-clot in the first aid kit on the houseboat. Sounds like you'll need some for Sandra, and we'll need some for Gary, too."

"I already got it out of your boat. Just get him here."

"Six minutes, Rik."

I didn't start pulling the throttles back until I was entering our inlet. The wake that I was throwing cleared the top of the jetty ends. I was coming in hot, with a *lot* of boat. At least I had lowered the pilot-house lights, so I could see the dock, but that didn't keep me from hitting it hard, broadside. Rik, Linds, Dawn, and Deputy Canfield were waiting at the end of the tee for us. Linds and Dawn got us secured while Canfield and Rik came running up to the bridge. Canfield unlocked first Gary's and then his crewmates' handcuffs while Rikki used the field clotting agent on Gary. A minute later Dawn led paramedics up to Gary. They strapped him on a backboard and carried him downstairs and to a wheeled gurney on the dock. After they loaded him into their truck, it screamed through the parking lot, lights and siren already going.

Canfield led us all off the boat since it was a crime scene. It turned out the Contender was too. When Marty was spraying the salon with bullets and wiping out the glass bulkhead, one of the bullets managed to lodge itself in the console. Linds ended up getting some fiberglass fragments in her right arm when they splintered and flew out the empty hole for the flatscreen. She was lucky. Hell, we all were lucky.

As more sheriff's cars rolled into the driveway, I knew this was going to be a very long night for all of us.

EPILOGUE

It was a little over a week after the shootings. I was having a Chuck's Martini onboard *OCT* with Lindsay when I got a video call from Sandy. He and Micah had made it to Islamorada where friends were asking if the shootout in Virginia hadn't been at his marina. He freaked out when he heard the name *Mallard Cove*, and I was calming him down.

"So, that's what happened, Sandy. Gary is scheduled to be released tomorrow, and Sandra got out a few days ago. Carlton's boatyard is doing a great job fixing up *Privacy*, she'll be good as new."

"Tell me you're not going to let it stay there!"

"Actually yes, we are. We all talked it over, and Sandra's not as bad as her father was, and certainly not as bad as her brother. She already stopped the Mystic Water distribution and production, though she's going to keep selling the prayer cubes until they're all gone. At least people know what they are getting with those. And she's buying back their old show from the bank that's foreclosing on it. While she still believes in the basic premise of the prosperity gospel, she's going to start a ministry helping unaffiliated rural churches that have fallen on hard times as Rev's had. It'll give them funds to do repairs and improvements, but with no strings attached. So, she's changed a bit, too. She stopped in to pray with Gary several times, and he's sticking with her when he's able to get back to work. She's still paying him while he's out."

Sandy said, "I'm surprised she wants to keep that boat, after everything bad that happened aboard her."

"Well, she's got me quietly looking for a slightly smaller one, if somebody is willing to do a swap. I'll find her something once the news finally settles down."

"And they never found the brother's body?"

I shook my head. "Water's too cold. He'll probably pop up in the spring. Then again, we all thought he was done last time. Which is partly what helped keep me and Casey out of jail for taking matters into our own hands. That, and the fact there would have been four bodies instead of one if we hadn't stopped him. The cops and the Coasties would've never made it there in time.

"But about Marty, yeah, I got at least three slugs in him, and Casey swears he hit him more than that. But time will tell. Or not. Won't bother me any way it turns out, I'll still sleep at night. Oh, and we closed on that Gwynn's Island property two days ago. Kari is already getting her contractors together for it, starting with the marina. We won't make this next wedding season, but we'll be ready for the fall rockfish fishermen."

As I watched Sandy, I saw him wince, and a gray/green/black tabby cat appeared in his frame with him. "What the hell is that?"

He grinned. "His name is KC Shaw, and he's from Ocracoke Island. And he's a story for another day, which will have to wait until we get back up there in the spring to tell it.

"Well, I'm just glad you guys are all okay. It'd get boring around there without you. I can't wait to get back up there and help deplete your beer supply."

"Ah, yes. Baloney has been warning that I need to lay in a fresh stock. Filming ends at the end of this month."

"You tell that damn Gilligan to stay away from my supply! We're going to need a ton of it to get caught up when I get back there."

I said, "No doubt. Well, you take it easy, and we'll be watching for you after the spring thaw."

"You guys, too. I'm glad you're not dead."

I chuckled as I broke the connection. I really like Sandy, he's one of a kind.

OH, and I was right. Marty's cold water semi-preserved body washed up on the beach at Corolla, North Carolina the week before Sandy got back. Turns out that Casey and I tied after all for marksmanship. Marty had been dead before he hit the water.

Your favorites from Mallard Cove will return soon in COASTAL CURSE, book 8 of the Coastal Adventure Series.
Thanks for reading COASTAL CULPRIT!

AUTHOR'S NOTES

Thanks for reading **Coastal Culprit**! If you read this one before reading the other books in this series, don't worry. While it's better if they are read in sequence, each can still be read as a "stand-alone" book with a minimum of "spoilers". I used the phrase *that's a story for another day* to refer to things that were covered more in-depth in those other volumes.

Hey, if you liked **Coastal Culprit**, I'd appreciate it if you would leave a review on Goodreads.com or Book Bub. Just a line or two would be great! And I'd love to hear what you thought of it. You can reach me at contact@donrichbooks.com

I also have a private **Reader's Group** where once a month I share the pictures and stories that inspired the books. Members also get advance notice of any upcoming releases at discounted rates. You can sign up for the **Reader's Group** on my website, http://www.donrichbooks.com

Thanks again!
    Don Rich

GLOSSARY OF NAUTICAL TERMS

I grew up on the water in South Florida, and I have an extensive boating background. I've worked on boats, built them, rebuilt them, and spent a good amount of time in boat yards. I've always loved boats, and ever since I was a pre-teenager, I haven't gone longer than six months without owning at least one. Most of my friends are boaters, too. So it's easy for me to forget that not everyone is as familiar with the jargon as my friends and me, which is something that I've now been reminded of on more than one occasion. (My apologies to those readers that I ended up sending to the dictionary!) To make amends, here's a (growing) list of uniquely nautical terms and words that have been included in several of my books. Bear in mind that these definitions are based on my usage and experience. Things can be different from one region to another. For instance, you can fish for stripers in Montauk, New York, but here in Virginia, we fish for rockfish. But the true name for the target species is "striped bass."

So, here are the definitions of some of the more confusing words, at least as I know them. We'll start with a half dozen simple ones, then move on to those that are more complex:

- **Bow:** the front of the boat.
- **Stern:** back of the boat.
- **Port:** the left side of the boat.
- **Starboard:** the right side of the boat.
- **Aft:** the rear of the boat.
- **Forward:** (fore) the front of the boat.
- **Bow Thruster:** a propeller in a tube that is mounted from side to side through the bow below the waterline, allowing the captain more maneuverability and control when docking especially in adverse winds and currents. Powered by an electric or hydraulic motor.
- **Bulkhead:** boat wall.
- **Center Console:** a type of boat with a raised helm console in the middle of the boat with space on each side to walk around. Most also incorporate a built-in bench seat or cooler seat in the front.
- **Chine:** The longitudinal area running fore and aft where the bottom meets the side. It can be rounded or "sharp." They hurt when the boat rocks and it meets your head when you are swimming next to it. Trust me on that.
- **Circle Hook:** a fishhook designed to get caught in the corner of a fish's mouth. Greatly reduces the mortality of fish that are released or that break the line.
- **Citation:** at an airport, it's a type of jet made by Cessna. But here in Virginia, it's a slip of paper suitable for framing, issued by the state confirming that you caught a fish that's considered large for its particular species. Or it can be a speeding ticket, either on water or land. I like the fish kind better.
- **Covering Board:** a flat surface at the top of a gunwale usually made out of teak or fiberglass, that's used as a step for boarding and for mounting recessed rod holders.
- **Deck:** what floors on boats are called.

- **Fighting Chair:** a specialized chair that can be turned to face a fish. Mounted on a sturdy stanchion with a built-in gimbal, the chair allows the angler to use the attached footrest to use their legs and body to gain more leverage on a large fish. Most of today's fighting chairs are based on the design by my late friend John Rybovich.
- **Fish Box:** a built-in storage box for the day's catch. They can be mounted either elevated in the stern, or in the deck with a flush-mounted lid. Some of the higher-end sportfish boats have cooling systems or automatic ice makers that continually add ice throughout the trip.
- **Fishing Cockpit:** the lower aft deck on a sport fisherman that usually contains a fighting chair, fish box, baitwell, and tackle center. Surrounded on three sides by the gunwales and the stern. The cockpit deck is usually just above the waterline, with scuppers that drain overboard. Can get flooded when backing down hard on a big fish.
- **Flying Bridge (Flybridge):** a permanently mounted helm area on top of the wheelhouse. Can be open or enclosed.
- **Following Sea:** when the waves are moving toward the boat from behind the stern.
- **Gaff:** a large, usually barbless hook at the end of a pole, used for landing fish. They come in different sizes and lengths.
- **Gangway (Gangplank):** a removable ramp or set of stairs attached to the side of larger boats to allow easier access for boarding from a dock. Usually hinged to allow for tide variation.
- **Gear:** marine transmission which has forward, neutral, and reverse.
- **Gimbal:** there are a few types, but the ones in my books are rod holders with swivels built into fighting chairs.
- **Gin Pole:** a vertical pole next to the gunwale usually rigged with a block and tackle and used for hauling large

fish aboard. These used to be quite common until John Rybovich invented the transom door fifty years ago.

- **Gunwale (pronounced gun-null):** aft side area of a boat above the waterline, also the area on either side of a fishing cockpit.
- **Hatch:** a hole in a deck or bulkhead with a cover that may be hinged or completely removable. On a sport fisherman, the door into the wheelhouse may be called either a hatch or a door.
- **Head:** a bathroom, or a marine toilet.
- **Helm:** the area that includes the steering and engine controls. In many sportfishing boats, the controls are mounted on a helm pod, a wood box with radiused edges that juts out of a cabinet or bulkhead.
- **Keys Conch:** a person born in the Florida Keys. You can be born in Miami and move to the Keys an hour later, then live down there the rest of your life, and you will still NEVER be a Conch. They are usually very tough and independent characters.
- **Lean Seat:** a high bench seat usually found behind the helm of a center console. Designed to be leaned against or sat upon. May have storage built-in under the seat section.
- **Mezzanine Deck:** a shallow, raised deck on a sportfish just forward of the fishing cockpit, and aft of the wheelhouse bulkhead. Usually contains aft-facing bench seating for anglers to comfortably watch the baits that are being trolled behind the boat.
- **Outriggers:** long aluminum poles on sportfishing boats that are raked up and aft from up alongside the wheelhouse. They are extended outward when fishing, having clips on lines that carry the fishing lines out away from the boat, creating a wider spread.
- **Pilot Boat:** a smaller boat designed to handle all kinds of seas, whose sole purpose is delivering and retrieving a

captain with extensive local knowledge to larger boats approaching or leaving a port.

- **Rod Holder:** As the name suggests, a device that a fishing rod butt is inserted into to hold it steady. There are recessed types that are mounted in covering boards, and exposed ones attached to railings or tower legs.
- **Salon:** a living room area of a boat's cabin.
- **Scuppers:** deck or cockpit drains.
- **SeaKeeper Gyro:** a stabilizing gyro that almost eliminates roll in boats.
- **Shaft:** attaches a propeller to the gear.
- **Sheer Line:** the rail edge where the foredeck meets the side of the hull.
- **Sonar/Fish Finder:** electronic underwater 'radar' that displays the sea floor, and anything between it and the boat.
- **Sportfisherman (Sportfish):** a unique style of boat designed specifically for fishing.
- **Spread:** the arrangement of the baits being towed while trolling.
- **Stem:** the forwardmost edge of the bow.
- **Stern:** the farthest aft part of the boat, also called the transom.
- **Tackle Center:** a cabinet in the fishing cockpit or the center console which holds hooks, swivels, leads, and other fishing supplies.
- **(Tuna) Tower:** an aluminum pipe structure located above the house or the flybridge designed to hold spotters or riders, and may or may not have an additional helm.
- **Transom:** stern.
- **Transom (Tuna) Door:** a door in the stern just above the waterline, designed for boating large fish, but also useful for retrieving swimmers and divers.
- **Trough:** the lowest point between waves.

- **Wheel (Propeller):** slang for a prop.
- **Wheel (Steering):** controls the boat's direction.
- **Wheelhouse (House):** the cabin section of a boat which sometimes contains an enclosed helm.

ABOUT THE AUTHOR

Don Rich is the author of the bestselling Coastal Adventure Series. Three of his books even simultaneously held the top three spots in Amazon's Hot New Releases in Boating.

Don's books are set mainly in the mid-Atlantic because of his love for this stretch of the Atlantic coastline. A fifth-generation Florida native who grew up on the water, he has spent a good portion of his life on, in, under, or beside it.

He now makes his home in central Virginia. When he's not writing or watching another fantastic mid-Atlantic sunset, he can often be found on the Chesapeake Bay or the Atlantic Ocean with a fishing rod in his hand.

ALSO BY DON RICH

Check my website www.DonRichBooks.com for the current list of all my book titles.

The Coastal Beginnings Series:

(The prelude to the Coastal Adventure Series)

- COASTAL CHANGES
- COASTAL TREASURE
- COASTAL RULES
- COASTAL BLUFFS

The Coastal Adventure Series:

- COASTAL CONSPIRACY
- COASTAL COUSINS
- COASTAL PAYBACKS
- COASTAL TUNA
- COASTAL CATS
- COASTAL CAPER
- COASTAL CULPRIT
- COASTAL CURSE
- COASTAL JURY
- COASTAL CURRENCY
- COASTAL CRUISE

Other Books by Don Rich:

- GhostWRITER

Here's A Tropical Authors Novella by Deborah Brown, Nicholas Harvey, and Don Rich:

- **Priceless**

Go to my website at www.DonRichBooks.com for more information about joining my **Reader's Group**! And you can follow me on Facebook at: https://www.facebook.com/DonRichBooks

I'm also a member of TropicalAuthors.com, where you can find my latest books and those by dozens of my coastal writer friends!